# DREAMS TAKE FLIGHT

## BY JIM DALTON

# DREAMS TAKE FLIGHT

## BY JIM DALTON

ISBN: 061580554X
ISBN-13: 9780615805542

Library of Congress Control Number: 2013939628
Golden Bear Publishing Group
Chesterfield, Missouri

# CHAPTER ONE

## *Chance Meeting*

❧

It was a stormy day in St. Louis. Heavy thunderstorms began moving across the area in the midafternoon, with waves of storms continuing into the evening. Strong winds, hail, lightning, and several small tornados were spotted in the area. Since late afternoon, the airport had taken several direct hits, and had closed immediately following a complete power failure. Outbound flights were cancelled and inbound flights were diverted to other airports. Passengers and employees were told to vacate the airport proper and not to return until cleared to do so. Passengers were told to check in with their airline prior to returning to the airport. The power company said service would not be restored for at least twenty-four hours.

Lucas headed to the airport as much out of curiosity as out of feeling that it would be the right thing to do. To ignore his place of employment following a disaster seemed inappropriate and selfish. Not knowing what to expect, Lucas made his way to the airport. Along the way, he encountered numerous emergency vehicles. There were no lights to be seen, except those created by the occasional passing car. Limbs were down everywhere, sometimes even in the middle of the road. Lucas began to understand why people had been asked to stay off the streets.

Lucas arrived at the airport around 9:00 p.m. to find the facility completely dark. Another wave of rain had begun to pass through the area. He no sooner parked his car than the sky gave way to a downpour—a real monsoon.

Lucas jumped out of the car and dashed to the lobby door. He burst into the lobby as if he had been shot from a cannon. As soon as he made it inside, he heard a scream from the far side of the lobby.

"Who's there?" Lucas shouted.

"Autumn!" a woman shouted back. "Who are you and why are you here?"

"Lucas Sanders, pilot for State Side. I just wanted to come by and see whether anyone needed help. What are you doing here?" *Wonder why our sexy late night rep is here this time of the night much less now?*

"Heather asked me to cover for her tonight," Autumn replied. "Once everyone was told to go home I thought I should stay around to see if anything came up. For all I knew we might have an arrival or two. No one told me anything. Then the big storm hit, and I was afraid to leave."

"Where are you?"

"In the corner, by the coffee pots."

Being a fan of coffee, Lucas had no trouble making his way to Autumn, even in the total darkness of Gold Coast Aviation's lobby.

"How long have you been here?" he asked her.

"I took Heather's shift at two o'clock and have been here ever since. The bad storms hit right after two, and everyone left around five."

"So you've been here by yourself since five?" he asked.

"Yes, and I'm sorry I stayed."

"Have you eaten anything?"

"Just whatever I could find—mostly snack food."

*That rain and wind are really something,* Lucas thought to himself. *I wonder if the storm-warning sirens are working.*

Knowing that Autumn hadn't eaten for some time, and that food might help relieve some of her anxiety, Lucas decided to see what he could find.

"Autumn, I'm not sure what I can find, but I'll check the flight office to see whether there's something to eat in there. Be right back. Will you be OK?"

"I think so. With you here, I'm not so scared anymore."

*Poor girl, she is scared to death. Wonder what asshole just left her all alone? Probably some prick that only cared about himself. Someone should've gotten her out of here. Back to my current mission—finding something to eat. If there isn't anything in the flight office, I could always find something in one of the planes.*

After about fifteen minutes, Lucas returned to the area staked out by Autumn. He'd found a flashlight, and when he illuminated the area, Lucas could see that Autumn was upset. He sat down beside her and gave her shoulders a big bear hug. Lucas could see and feel her shivering.

"Are you cold?" he asked.

"No, I don't think so. I'm just scared, hungry, and nervous."

"If you're hungry, you can't be too scared," Lucas said with an upbeat tone.

Her hands were laced together between her legs. In a comforting voice, Lucas told Autumn that everything would be OK. He continued to hold Autumn, and felt her begin to relax.

"Autumn," he finally said. "I have good news and I have bad news. Which do you want first?"

"I'm already a nervous wreck. I don't think I could take any more bad news," Autumn replied.

"Have you been on the couch all this time?"

"Yes. I didn't know where else to go."

"Autumn, I want you to relax. What you are hearing outside is heavy rain and wind, but the severe weather is gone—it won't hurt either of us. The biggest problem is that power won't be restored until tomorrow morning, close to noon. Want to hear the better news?"

"If that's the good news, I'm not so sure. If it's really better, then I'm all for hearing anything."

"Well, last night I flew back from Chicago on the bird out front, and our passengers turned out to be executives coming home. One of their requests was to have food available following their meeting—you know, something to eat on their way home. So we had the fridge full of sandwiches and pizza. Best of all, their meeting apparently didn't go well and no one ate anything."

By this point, Autumn had stopped shaking and was developing a real interest in what Lucas had to say.

"So let's go raid the fridge," she said.

"That's exactly what I was thinking. You put my raincoat over your head and hang on to it so the wind doesn't blow it away, and we'll make a dash to the plane."

"We have to go outside in this stuff?" Terror returned to Autumn's voice.

"It'll be OK. I promise. Grab your flashlight and let's run for it."

Lucas and Autumn sprinted to the plane that had been tied down about 300 feet in front of the office. Autumn ran under the wing while Lucas lowered the stairs. As soon as the stairs reached the ramp, Autumn made a beeline to the open door with Lucas in hot pursuit. Once inside, Lucas wasted no time in raising the stairs and securing the door.

Their temporary shelter was an ex-airliner that had been converted into an executive aircraft with a seating capacity of eighteen people. Most of the seating was in the aft cabin, where several couches and swivel chairs were located. About midway through the aft cabin was a bar and entertainment center. The forward cabin was an executive office suite with an attractive desk, an oversized love seat, and two swivel chairs. A galley, complete with a microwave oven, and refrigerator, separated the executive office and the cockpit.

"Autumn, give me the raincoat and I'll hang it up in the shower where it can dry. While you're at it, why don't you take your shoes off and let them dry? I'll be right back."

"Are you telling me there is a shower in the back of this plane?"

"Sure is. These corporate airplanes are well-equipped."

"No kidding."

"You've never been in any of these planes?"

"No," said Autumn, "but I think I've been missing something."

"In the next few days, I'll make it a point to give you a grand tour of the planes that provide you with a job. You should be familiar with the birds your customers are flying."

"Thanks, Lucas; I'd appreciate that. I also want to thank you for staying with me tonight. I don't know what I would've done if you hadn't shown up."

"I'm just glad I did. I feel terrible that you were alone for as long as you were." Lucas paused and then said, "Give me just a few more minutes. I'm going to turn the plane's generator on and then I'll make you something to eat and drink. Here, take this blanket and wrap it around yourself; in no time you'll feel like you're sitting in your living room."

"Thanks. This blanket feels good."

"Incidentally, I don't want to turn the cabin lights on—you know, call attention to us. Let's just use the flashlight."

Autumn nodded and looked around the cabin. "This isn't a big deal," she said, "but I don't think I'm ever going to believe that this is my living room."

"Why is that?"

"This furniture is too nice for my living room."

Lucas laughed. "Come on!" he said. "Now, what would you like to eat? I have sub sandwiches or an individual pizza."

"How about a sandwich?"

"One gourmet sandwich coming right up. What would you like to drink? I have whatever you might want in the bar."

"A glass of white wine would hit the spot."

"Autumn, one white wine and that sandwich will be ready shortly."

In just a few minutes, Lucas returned with a tray containing several sandwiches, potato chips, a glass of wine and a bottle of beer. He'd found an assortment of chocolates for dessert.

Autumn sat on the floor of the executive office, leaning against the love seat. Lucas handed the tray to her as he lowered himself to the floor, facing her. Autumn positioned the tray off to the side, within reach of both. They each took a sandwich and helped themselves to their drinks. The rain and wind were loud, and the light on the inside was subdued, creating an alluring atmosphere.

"Lucas, this is breathtaking," said Autumn. "Just a short while ago I was petrified by this storm. Thanks to you, I'm warm, eating a feast created for powerful people, and enjoying a wonderful glass of wine, all in the company of a cool guy."

"Cool guy?' Don't know what you're selling, but I'm buying. Glad you're feeling better. Hear the rain? It's really coming down. This reminds me of when I was a kid and would spend the night at my uncle's farm. He had a tin roof, and thunderstorms sounded exactly like this. Funny how little things will sometimes trigger certain memories."

"With you here, the rain sounds relaxing. Was that the case when you were a kid?"

"Exactly. I remember the sound of the rain as it created this calming rhythm on the roof that would lull me to sleep in no time." Lucas's voice grew lower as he reminisced.

"So what's with you and Heather?" Autumn asked.

"Nothing. Why do you ask?"

"According to Heather, she has this thing for you."

"I've heard that before. She may have a thing for me, but I've hardly spoken to her, much less have a thing for her."

"So you two aren't a thing?"

"Absolutely not. I'm not dating anyone."

"No one?"

"You got it."

"Are you gay?"

"No, I'm not gay. I just haven't had time for romance."

"So you're available?

"I guess technically I'm available, but I'm not looking."

"Just curious. Is there more wine?"

"Sure, I'll go get the bottle."

Returning with a bottle of white wine for Autumn and a bottle of red wine for himself, Lucas maneuvered to sit directly in front of Autumn.

"Autumn, if you hand me your glass, I'll give you a fill-up."

"Forget the glass; just give me the bottle. You don't mind if I drink from the bottle, do you?"

"You go for it."

"We're not going to get into trouble for being here and drinking the company's booze, are we?"

"No. This won't be the first time the liquor cabinet has been raided. In light of the weather, I don't think anyone will mind, but I would prefer that we leave here by sunrise tomorrow."

Autumn realized that his statement was another way of saying they were spending the night together. Her imagination kicked into high gear. She couldn't help but wonder whether Lucas had some sort of agenda for the night, or was just being nice. She hadn't had a steady boyfriend for some time, and thought this might be one of those once-in-a-lifetime opportunities with fate working in her favor. Autumn needed to find a way to discover what was on Lucas's mind. Recognizing that romance could be in her future, she began to take inventory of her attire. *Hair is a mess from running through the rain, makeup is mostly a mess, skirt and blouse are OK—not what I would've picked for a date, but attractive. Had I known I would be spending the night with a guy, I would have chosen a skirt an inch or two shorter, but I didn't, so this one will have to do.*

"Why were you covering for Heather tonight?" Lucas asked.

"She had a family reunion out of town or something like that."

"I was just curious," said Lucas. "We don't see you very often. I guess you're getting to work at about the time we're heading out for the night."

"Now I understand," said Autumn. "You came to the airport tonight to rescue Heather."

"No, not at all. I already told you there isn't anything between Heather and me. I came to the airport tonight to see if there was anything I could help with."

"So you're serious? You and Heather aren't a thing?"

"Yep. I just know her from the airport and don't even talk to her very often."

"I'm getting low on my wine. Where can I find another bottle? Can I bring you something?" Autumn asked.

"I'll take a bottle of red wine and I'll take your no-glass approach. In fact, I'll get it."

"No, Lucas. Stay put; you've done enough for me tonight. The least I can do is get you a bottle of someone else's wine. Also, I need to pee. Where's the bathroom on this plane?"

"The bathroom is straight back and the bar is just beyond this partition, on the left side," Lucas said, gesturing.

"Can I borrow the flashlight? Don't need it to pee, just want to make sure I get the right wine."

"Sure, but peeing in the right spot isn't all bad either."

"Cute, Lucas, but I don't have the same problem you have."

"All right."

Autumn went directly to the restroom, leaving Lucas in the dark. Without the distraction of Autumn, Lucas was reminded of the thunderstorm taking place outside. The strong wind buffeted the plane, reminding Lucas that he wasn't in a solid structure. The rain came down in buckets, the lightning seemed brighter and the thunder seemed louder than before. As a pilot, his senses were keen when it came to thunderstorms. Lucas's thoughts began to shift from the weather to Autumn and what kind of sleeping arrangements they could make.

Autumn found the restroom and after a badly needed pee, decided to tip the scale in her favor. Lucas had mentioned he wasn't looking for romance, but he didn't say that he would turn his head if it were presented to him. On her way back to the executive compartment, Autumn stopped at the bar and retrieved a bottle of red and a bottle of white wine.

As Autumn entered the executive compartment, Lucas sprung to his feet to take the bottle of red wine and the flashlight she had tucked under her right arm. With the aid of Lucas and the flashlight, Autumn managed to return to her original resting place. Lowering herself to the floor with her right hand leaning on the couch, she folded her legs to the left with her knees pointing toward Lucas. Lucas returned to his previous position with his legs stretched out pointing toward the cockpit, his head resting on his right hand while his right elbow leaned against a swivel chair across the aisle from the couch. He set the flashlight down halfway between himself and Autumn, pointing it toward the ceiling. The light reflecting off the ceiling gave the cabin a warm glow. Once settled, Lucas uncorked the wine and the two indulged themselves in idle conversation and an abundant supply of alcohol.

"So Lucas, tell me about yourself. Who are you?"

"I don't usually talk about myself," Lucas said. "Why do you ask?"

"I would just like to know a little bit about the guy I'm about to spend the night with."

"I understand when you put it like that, but we're not exactly *spending the night together.* This is more like…sharing the same shelter."

"Call it what you will, but to me we're spending the night together. Now stop being a tight ass and tell me who you are."

"Persistent, aren't you?" he teased.

"I have my moments."

"Well, I started flying for State Side about seven years ago. When I got this job, I had a little more than a year left of school, but my flying schedule made it nearly impossible to stay in school, so I quit. Seven years later, I'm now back in school and will finish my degree when I finish the summer session."

"What's your major?"

"Psychology."

"Are you going to do anything with it?"

"Not really, but I was so close it didn't make sense not to finish. Most importantly, major airlines require a degree and I've wanted to work for a major carrier for years. In fact, I have a standing offer from Global once I finish school."

"So, why no girlfriend?"

"Why the third degree?"

"I already told you; I want to know more about the person I'm spending the night with—or, as you put it, *sharing the same shelter with*."

"All right," he said, with an edge in the tone of his voice. "I don't have time. I fly almost every night and go to school during the day. Women just don't fit into my schedule right now."

"Do you have any hobbies?"

"I have a boat, but seldom get to take it out. Beyond that, I enjoy working out. I want to stay healthy. You know, physically fit."

"I like guys that are physically fit."

Autumn could sense that the conversation was slowing and felt like the time was right to give Lucas something to think about. Having consumed more than a tall bottle of wine, Autumn felt a little bold, if not downright forward.

"Lucas, let's fuck."

"What?"

"You heard me. Let's get it on. You know: you put your thing in my thing."

"I know what it is and where everything goes, but I don't understand."

"We're stuck here for the night; what else do we have to do? Play cards? Besides, you already told me you don't have a girlfriend."

"I don't, and I'm not looking for one either."

"I didn't say let's start dating. I said let's get it on, no strings attached. Let's just see if we can enjoy a fun night of sex. Ever hear of recreational sex?"

"I have."

"Well, I'm up for a little recreation."

While selling her proposition, Autumn slowly but deliberately began to unbutton her blouse. As Lucas's body language and look made it apparent that he was receptive to her suggestion, she began to proceed more quickly.

"I like the idea, but what about tomorrow?" Lucas asked.

"We can do it again tomorrow if you like."

"That's not what I'm talking about. How will you feel tomorrow?"

"Like I've died and gone to heaven."

"Autumn, cut it out. You know what I'm talking about."

"Fuck tomorrow. Don't worry about it, Lucas. Let's throw caution to the wind and just enjoy the night."

"OK. I'm game if you are, if you really mean what you're saying."

"Stop talking and get those pants off."

The rain continued to fall with an overdose of wind, lightning, and thunder. The rain was loud, only silenced by the occasional, overpowering sound of thunder. Despite being tied down, the plane continued to shake from the relentless wind—a reminder that regardless of what took place inside the plane, there was a mean thunderstorm taking place outside.

Autumn removed her white sleeveless blouse and tossed it to the far corner of the couch, followed by her bra. Exhibiting more grace than he expected the wine to allow, she stood, swaying slightly in time with the pulsing rain. Her skirt fell to the floor with a quick pull on her zipper, exposing her silk, white bikini panties. With a seductive look, Autumn, with a thumb inserted in each side of her panties began to slide them down slowly and deliberately. Once they were within a few inches of the floor, she stepped out of them while never breaking eye contact with Lucas. Her beautiful, soft body was exposed in the warm glow of the flashlight. Lucas couldn't take his eyes off Autumn. She just stood there with her hands on her hips and legs spread apart. Her look was seductive. Autumn was a beautiful woman with a special radiance about her. She stood five-feet, seven-inches tall with her weight in proportion to her height. Her figure was near perfect. Autumn's hands were petite and well cared for. Her black hair extended beyond her shoulders and her skin was blemish-free, with a healthy looking tan. Her face was covered with a generous supply of freckles, which added to her innocent look. Her pubic area has been trimmed to accommodate a skimpy bikini. In that moment, her nipples puckered firm and erect.

Lucas found himself mesmerized by the sight of Autumn without a stitch of clothes on. This beautiful woman stood just inches away, with two beautiful legs leading to a perfect "V" of pubic hair, marking the location of a warm and inviting source of pleasure. Lucas felt as though this couldn't be real. *Why would a perfect "10" be seducing me*, he wondered. Just the sight of Autumn had him excited.

"OK, big boy, your turn," she said. "Drop your drawers. Let's see what you've got."

"OK, but I'm warning you: you'd best stand back."

"Don't tell me about it; show me."

Lucas hurriedly stripped off his shirt, followed by his fly unbuttoned, zipper down, and pants flung out of sight all within the blink of an eye, a reflection of his heightened state of excitement. With his right hand, he pulled his briefs down while stepping out of them, and used his left foot to toss them away. Standing there, bare-ass naked, his dick was hard and erect, like a missile ready to seek out that target a mere three feet away.

Lucas and Autumn moved toward each other until Lucas's dick pressed against Autumn's belly. Their shared body heat caused their senses to reach new heights. They embraced, each pulling the other closer, both of their hands cupping the other's buttocks. Their mouths hungrily sought one another, tongues eagerly explored each other as they kissed long and heavy. Lucas could feel his dick throb as their gentle movements caused him to want to bury himself deep in Autumn. As their kisses became more passionate, Lucas began to explore Autumn's body. With his left hand cupping her buttocks, his right hand rubbed her between her legs where he found her warm and silky smooth.

To avoid climaxing, he had to shift his thoughts from his own pleasure to Autumn's. Lucas began to lower himself. He paused for a gentle caress of her nipples—first the right and then the left. Her breasts were soft and firm, her nipples hard and erect. Using his tongue, he circled each nipple, ending with a gentle suck. As Lucas slowly lowered himself, his dick slid down and teased the area where Autumn's legs met. He was still hard and throbbing. While playing with Autumn's nipples, his dick toyed with the moistness between her legs. The teasing of Autumn's pussy caused Lucas's focus to shift to his dick, poised to seek out the depths of her offering. Lucas continued to lower his lips to Autumn's stomach, pausing only long enough to kiss her belly button.

Autumn stood with her legs spread ever so slightly. Her hands fondled Lucas's hair for lack of any other part of Lucas to play with. Her head tipped back and she moaned as Lucas explored the curves of her body. Lucas, on his knees, began to kiss her pubic area while massaging the backs of her legs. With his right hand, Lucas reached around and began to play with her warm, soft, and moist lips. Her wetness was silky smooth. Lucas inserted a finger just deep enough to elicit a response. He continued to use his finger to fuck her slowly and gently. With each movement of his finger, Autumn moaned and began to touch her own breasts. Lucas's dick became so hard it began to hurt, as if about to explode. Both he and Autumn approached climax.

"Autumn, let's move to the couch."

"I thought you'd never ask. Not that I'm complaining."

Autumn sprawled out, with her head on the arm of the couch, her right leg hanging off the edge and her left foot resting on the back of the couch. This position left her wide open and inviting. Lucas wasted no time positioning himself between her legs. His dick slid in easily. Autumn arched her back, allowing him to penetrate even deeper. Lucas began thrusting in and out; both breathed hard until they simultaneously exploded in ecstasy. Neither could move. They held each other tightly as they regained control of their feelings and bodies.

Lucas slowly withdrew and leaned back against the other arm of the couch. His breathing began to return to normal as his entire body went limp—except for his dick, which remained hard and erect. Autumn just lay there as she recovered, legs still wide open.

"Lucas, I thought you were going to kill me. I think this has been the best sex ever."

"When I came to the airport tonight, I had no idea you and I would be having sex before sunrise. Autumn, you were fantastic."

"*We* were fantastic," corrected Autumn.

"Autumn, the storm is still crazy outside. Why don't we nap before we get our things together and bail?"

"I don't know if it's you or the wine, but I feel like I could sleep forever," remarked Autumn.

"It's probably the wine, but I'm OK with taking the credit."

"Typical guy!"

"Hey, Autumn; you're the one that suggested we do the deed."

"Aren't you glad? Truth is, you get the credit. I am totally relaxed."

"I'm glad. Still surprised, but glad."

The two fell asleep with Lucas leaning against one arm of the couch and Autumn against the other. Lucas's legs hung off the couch, his left foot on the floor and his right leg dangling. His right arm stretched out so that his hand rested softly on Autumn's wetness. Autumn's right leg hung over Lucas's legs; her left leg was bent, foot resting on the couch.

As the sun began to rise, the cabin appeared to come to life. All the shades were still open. Lucas woke up first. Both he and Autumn were still in the same position they were in when they fell asleep.

Lucas looked toward Autumn and could see his dick looking back. It was hard and ready for action. Autumn was still asleep. Her legs were spread apart, leaving her exposed and inviting. Her breasts appeared firm and perfectly shaped. Her look and posture were stimulating, causing Lucas to become aroused. Lucas looked at his watch and concluded that they had about an hour and a half before they needed to leave.

Outside, the rain continued to pour, but the lightning and thunder had faded into the distance. The sun played behind clouds that seemed reluctant to give up their hold on the St. Louis area. Lucas took a long look at Autumn, thinking that there was no way he could get up and put his pants on without fucking her. Whatever concern he had about Autumn thinking he might be available for a relationship disappeared as his dick began to throb.

Lucas began to rub the inside of Autumn's left leg. Feeling her soft skin and seeing her open to the world had him excited. He leaned slightly forward so he could also see her warm, moist lips as he continued to explore her body. Autumn began to wake up as his fingers toyed with her thighs and the softness between her legs. She smiled, stretching out both arms as she yawned widely. Returning her outstretched right hand to his dick and her left hand to Lucas's mischievous and roaming right hand, she carefully moved his hand to her silky wetness and held it there while she stroked his dick.

"Lucas, how much time do we have?"

"About an hour and a half."

"In that case, I'm going to fuck you like you've never been fucked. Come up here, big boy."

Lucas and Autumn unraveled themselves, with her remaining on her side of the couch, lying down. Her head rested on the arm of the couch, her right leg hanging off the couch and her left leg again braced on the top of the couch. Lucas carefully positioned his dick between Autumn's legs and lowered himself to lick and suck her left breast.

While caressing her breast, his dick teased her as it brushed against the softest, smoothest, most sensitive part of her body. Lucas's hands cupped Autumn's shoulders. As his attention shifted from her left breast to her left ear and neck, his dick entered Autumn, but only partially. His warmth, his manly scent, his dick barely inside her, drove Autumn over the edge. No longer able to control herself, she pulled Lucas deep inside her. As he entered, Autumn felt a sudden burst of energy, causing her to arch her back while moving her hips up and down. Lucas reciprocated by thrusting his dick in and out of her, both of them out of control as they vigorously travelled to ecstasy. Suddenly, Autumn's body stiffened and she held Lucas tightly, announcing her orgasm. Lucas continued thrusting his dick in and out until that magical moment when he stopped abruptly and his dick fired deep inside Autumn. Both lay motionless, holding each other tightly. For the moment, they were both physically and emotionally exhausted.

They slowly and deliberately began to unravel and sit up to clear their heads. Sex and alcohol had obviously impacted their states of mind and levels of energy.

"Autumn, what do you think? Ready to get dressed and get out of here?"

"No," she said flatly. "I want to fuck some more, but I guess we have to."

"We should. The last I heard, the airport wouldn't have power until sometime around noon today, but who knows who might show up to assess the damage."

Autumn and Lucas began to sort out their clothes and put themselves back together to whatever extent possible. Once that was accomplished, their efforts shifted to the plane itself, their overnight cocoon. Everything appeared as they found it, allowing Lucas and Autumn to shift their attention to the beginning of a new day.

"So Autumn," asked Lucas, "what are you doing the rest of the day?"

"I'm going home, taking a shower, and seeing if I can't get some shut-eye. What are you doing?"

"About the same. I need to do some homework and eventually check in with flight ops to see what's going on this evening. About last night," he said after an awkward pause. "I hope you don't get the wrong impression."

"Hey," Autumn said. "*I* seduced *you*. I know you aren't looking for a relationship. Don't be concerned. We had a good fuck, nothing more."

"Glad you understand. Let's make sure we have everything before we split."

One last check of the plane convinced both that it was just as they'd found it, minus a little wine.

"Lucas," Autumn said. "Even though I seldom see you when you return from your evening trips, I know you usually get back before I get off work. I just want you to know that if you ever want a quick fuck with no strings attached, you should stop by the counter and let me know."

"I'll remember that, Autumn. I like that arrangement." After a short pause, Lucas added, "If you're ready to go, I'll open the door. Once the stairs hit the asphalt, you can make a dash to your car."

"I'm ready; let her go."

Lucas unlocked the door. As the stairs began to lower to the ground, he kissed Autumn on the head. She ran down the steps and jogged across the flight line, while giggling and making other childlike sounds until she disappeared around the corner of the hangar. Lucas checked the cabin one last time before descending the stairs himself. After confirming the stairs were properly stowed, Lucas also dashed to his car.

Lucas realized that he couldn't advance his flying career by sleeping around in corporate airplanes. He reflected on the evening with Autumn and knew that it was nothing more than his attempt to be of some assistance during a disaster, and that ultimately things got out of hand.

*I know I can't let anything interfere with my opportunity with Global,* he thought. *The solution: leave women alone and focus on school and my current flying job. There will be time for romance once I finish my flight training with Global.*

# CHAPTER TWO

## One For The Road

❧

E arly one morning, about week after his encounter with
Autumn, Lucas received a phone call from the hiring manager for Global Airlines.

"Lucas, this is Frank Morrison from Global Airlines. How are
you today?"

"I'm fine. How are you?" Wondering why Global would be
calling out of the blue, Lucas felt a rush of anxiety throughout
his body.

"Lucas, we've been fine-tuning our recruiting and training
plans for the balance of the year, and it looks like we may have
to delay your start date by as much as six months. Is that going
to create a problem for you?"

Taken by surprise, Lucas found himself unable to respond.

"Lucas," Frank said, "are you still there?"

"Oh, yes. You just took me by surprise; I wasn't expecting to
hear from you. Is there a problem? I thought everything was in
place for me to start once I graduate."

"That was the plan, but we were able to pick up six furloughed pilots from a small carrier in the Bahamas. They're already qualified to fly MD-80s, so we couldn't pass up the opportunity. Are you still flying for State Side?"

Lucas couldn't believe this was happening. His dream was collapsing with a single phone call. "Yes, I am."

"Still flying the Convair? How's the jet time?"

"Yes," said Lucas. "I'm still flying the Convair regularly, and on occasion I fly a King Air, Lear Jet, and a Cessna Citation. I have about 1,600 hours jet time and around 4,000 hours total time." The more they talked, the more concerned Lucas became. "Am I still being considered for a position?"

"Absolutely. We still want you to fly for Global, but with the competition you're faced with, it just looks like we may have to delay your start date."

"Is there anything I can do to maintain that original start date?"

"We have two seats still available in the class you're scheduled in, but Operations has asked us to hold those seats for pilots already qualified on MD-80s. That's the problem."

"Frank, what can I do? Is there anyone else I should talk with? Is there anything I can do?" Lucas was beginning to feel sick.

"Lucas, I understand your disappointment. Tell you what I'll do: I'll schedule you back for a follow-up interview with our chief of operations, and we'll see if he's willing to make an exception. How does that sound?"

"I'd like that. I've been planning everything around working for Global after graduation. I would still like to maintain that schedule."

"OK, Lucas," said Frank. "I'll be in touch with you soon. In the meantime, you keep your nose squeaky clean and we'll see if we can't get you in as scheduled. Take care. Talk to you soon."

"Thanks for your help, Frank. Talk to you later."

That evening, Lucas reached the airport at 9:00 p.m., his usual time of arrival. Following his standard flight procedure, Lucas proceeded to his assigned Convair and conducted a routine pre-flight check.

The plane's captain and Lucas's longtime partner, Mike "Shorty" Short, typically arrived around ten o'clock and headed directly to the flight office. Preflight completed and the Convair loaded, Lucas headed for the flight office to notify Mike that the plane was ready to go. Together, they left the office and headed for the Convair.

Once inside, Mike headed for the left seat and settled in, while Lucas raised the stairs and secured the cabin door. He took a moment to confirm the door was securely locked, and then proceeded to the cockpit. There, he settled into the copilot's seat on the right.

"Lucas, you want to take it to Omaha or bring it back?"

"Why don't I take the first leg and you bring it home?" Lucas said.

"Sounds like a plan," said Mike.

Mike handled the checklist and radio communications while Lucas served as the active pilot.

Mike: "Clearance, this is Convair three-seven-one-three-papa, I.F.R. Omaha."

Controller: "Convair three-seven-one-three-papa cleared as filed. Squawk zero-seven-four-seven; maintain six thousand. Departure one-one-nine-point-nine."

Mike: "Roger. One-three-papa cleared as filed. Squawk zero-seven-four-seven, maintain six and departure one-one-nine-point-nine."

Controller: "One-three-papa: read back correct contact ground when ready to taxi."

Mike: "One-three-papa."

Mike proceeded through the checklist, calling out the various items to be checked. Lucas responded, appropriately confirming flight readiness. Once they reached the end of the checklist, Lucas fired up the engines and Mike called ground control to obtain their taxi clearance, which took them to runway one-two right.

Arriving at the departure end of runway one-two right, the Convair stopped on the run-up pad, where Mike took them through their final checklist prior to departure.

"What ya say, Lucas," he asked at the end. "Ready to roll?"

"Yep, let's bore a hole in the sky."

Mike called the tower, saying, "Tower, this is three-seven-one-three-papa ready to go on runway one-two right."

Controller: "Convair three-seven-one-three-papa cleared for takeoff, runway one-two right. Turn left three-four-zero, maintain six thousand."

Mike: "One-three-papa, left to three-four-zero, maintain six thousand."

Lucas pulled the Convair onto the runway and lined up along the centerline, and then slowly advanced the throttles to takeoff power while Mike followed the throttles forward with his right hand.

The Convair began to accelerate as Mike called out each speed. "There's V1," he said. "V2."

Shortly after hearing that V2 had been reached, Lucas pulled the wheel back. The Convair left the runway.

"We have a positive rate of climb; the gears are coming up," announced Mike. By that point, the Convair was fully airborne and en route to Omaha. As they reached the departure end of the runway, Lucas rolled the Convair into a left bank and turned to his assigned heading of three-four-zero. During this phase of the flight, both Lucas and Mike constantly scanned the outside environment for other traffic, without ever ignoring the various engine and flight instruments on the panel. Once Lucas reached his desired heading, he rolled the plane level while continuing their climb.

"Lucas, everything is still in the green," Mike said. "Water is off, boost pump off, flaps up, bypass up, cowl flaps going to mid."

Area cleared and the initial phase of the climb completed, Lucas took a moment to absorb and appreciate the strange and wonderful world he worked in. During the initial phase of the climb, Lucas always felt as though man and machine became one. As its huge engines strained to lift the heavy cargo and fuel load into the air, climbing slowly to a cruising altitude, the Convair always seemed to speak to him. It seemed to say, "I'll get the job done, but I'm not in a hurry to put thousands of feet between me and the ground." The message was subtle, but the sound of the engines and the vibration felt in the control wheel were both clear. The engines groaned against the weight, and the rate of climb remained slow as they passed over Florissant in north St. Louis County. Faint shadows, created by the lights below, moved across the overhead console, adding to the sensation of speed. With each passing mile, the shadows faded away, yielding to the warm, red glow of the cockpit light. All sense of speed disappeared, as did the ground, as the city fell away, leaving only dark, ill-defined farmland below.

Once their route was established, the conversation shifted from checklists, speeds, and headings to casual chitchat. For no special reason, Lucas decided that this would be an opportune time to find out more about his friend and flying partner. Although they'd flown together for several years, Lucas didn't know much about Mike. He'd learned about his life and interests only in small doses.

"So, Mike," Lucas said. "How did you get into this crazy business?"

"I never told you the story?"

"Nope."

"I wonder how you escaped it. Well, here is a shortened version: I had a friend named Alex back in college, and during our junior year Alex convinced me that we should both go into the Air Force when we graduated. That way we could go through training together and, we assumed, get assigned to the same base. Neither of us had any interest in flying, but we both thought that if we joined the service, the Air Force would be the best branch."

"Did it work out like you planned?" asked Lucas.

"Yes and no. We took all of the entrance tests and both did well enough that the recruiter encouraged us to pursue flying. We went through basic training, but when we took our physicals for flight training, Alex discovered he had a kidney problem. He not only wasn't allowed in flight school, he was discharged. A year later, I found myself in a war zone with everyone and his brother trying to shoot my ass out of the sky."

"Is that when you started drinking?"

With that question, Mike turned to face Lucas and glared in disapproval. Finally, he shifted his focus back to the instruments and said, "Why not? I still got the job done. My bombs hit their targets."

"Mike, I wasn't passing judgment, just asking. You and I have been flying together for a long time and it was apparent some time ago that you had a thing for the bottle. Anyway, you ever hear from Judy?"

"No, and that's OK by me. We didn't get along very well, and we both knew we were headed for divorce, but I just can't forgive her for leaving me while I was on a trip. Good riddance. Judy may have been number three, but there won't be a fourth."

"How long has it been?" Lucas asked. "Two years?"

"Bout that."

After a long silence, Lucas said, "It sounds like Global may delay my start date, but I don't want to talk about that now. I should know more in a few days."

"That would be unfortunate. Keep me posted."

With that, the conversation shifted from one subject to another, allowing a pleasant exchange for the balance of the trip.

Once they were back in St. Louis and the Convair put to bed, Mike and Lucas headed for the flight office to drop off the required paperwork. After turning it in, they immediately exited through the hanger door and headed for their cars. They'd just barely made it to the parking lot when Lucas stopped and announced that he had to run back in. *My going back in shouldn't suggest that I'm going to see Autumn. Even if he did find out, the world won't stop spinning.*

"Mike, I won't be but a minute, but there's no need for you to stick around; I'll see you tomorrow night."

"Don't stay up too late," responded Mike, smiling.

Having parted company with Mike, Lucas returned to the lobby through the hangar door. He could see Autumn sitting at the receptionist desk, back to him, and he revealed his presence with a subdued hello, hoping the warning would avoid startling her.

"Autumn, how you doing this morning?"

Autumn swung around to face Lucas, saying, "Well, it's three thirty in the morning and I'm by myself filing yesterday's fuel bills, sleepy, and bored. Otherwise I'm doing fine. What are you doing here?"

"Mike and I just got back from Omaha, and I thought I would stop by and say hello."

"I'm glad you did" with a smile that ran from one side of her face to the other. "This is a pleasant surprise."

"I was thinking about you and our encounter following the storm," Lucas said, "and just wanted to stop by. You've been on my mind lately. Doing OK?"

"Tell me, Lucas: what is on your mind? Are you looking for a repeat performance?"

"No, ah no. Like I said, I've just been thinking about you," with uncertainty in the tone of his voice. *Now I wonder if I did come back just for a quickie.*

"It's three thirty in the morning and you were just thinking about me? What were you thinking?"

With laughter in his voice, Lucas said, "Just that I hadn't seen you for a while and wanted to stop by and say hello."

"You want a little, don't you?"

"Well, I really hadn't thought about it until you mentioned it. I actually just stopped by to see how you were doing. But if you insist, you could probably talk me into it."

"Just as I thought. What are we going to do about that?"

"I hadn't thought about it, since I really did just stop by to say hello."

"Lucas, you're full of shit. Follow me." As Autumn rose from her seat, she motioned Lucas to follow her. She headed for the end of the counter, where the pass-through was located.

Autumn wore one of her usual miniskirts, so common among the customer service reps at Gold Coast. The skirt was a lightweight, navy-blue polyester. Her white blouse was cut low in the front, exposing significant cleavage. The color contrast between her blouse and skirt was striking, giving her an elegant look—one that would capture the attention of any guy. Her shoes were sandals more suitable for the beach than the office. She looked radiant and lively, unlike the last time she and Lucas had been together.

Lucas hadn't yet changed out of his short-sleeved uniform. *I can't believe this gal has any interest in me. She and Heather are the two most beautiful women I've ever met. And Autumn is so fresh and playful; no pretense to being innocent. With her looks and personality, I just can't figure out why some guy hasn't taken her off the market. A good romp between the sheets isn't everything, but whatever everything is, she seems to have it. Good thing I'm not on the prowl.*

"Where are you going?" asked Lucas.

"You'll see."

"Can you just leave the counter like this? What happens if the phone rings, or some inbound pilot gives you a call on the radio?"

"I will apologize with a smile and tell them I was in the restroom fucking you. That always stops people from asking more questions."

"Autumn," Lucas said in a stern voice. "I'm serious."

"And you think I'm not."

"Will you cut it out?"

"Relax. If someone calls, I will simply say I was in the restroom. People understand."

"All right, but what are we doing?"

"I'm going to give you what you came here for: a quickie for the road. You'll sleep better for it."

"You've already given me what I came here for."

"Sure," Autumn said, with a playful tone of agreement in her voice. "Just relax and follow me."

"Hang on, Autumn: you're taking me into the ladies room?"

"Will you just relax? Jeez, you're going to die a young man, Mr. Sanders, if you don't start relaxing." Autumn held the door open for Lucas, allowing him to enter first. "There won't be anyone here for hours," She added.

The restroom was relatively small, with four stalls, a double sink, and—near the sink but opposite the stalls—a six-foot-long bench with chrome legs. The bench was padded with a bright red, leather cushion. The top of it was elegantly tucked and rolled.

"Autumn," Lucas said, sounding doubtful. "Do you know what you're doing?"

"I'll let you be the judge. Now slip your shoes off and drop your pants—or am I going to have to undress you?"

Lucas sat down, took his shoes off, and slid them underneath the bench. Autumn sat down next to him and began to disrobe. Lucas got back to his feet to unzip his pants and slide them down to his ankles, along with his boxers. He stepped out of his pants with his right foot and tossed them next to the sink with his left. Autumn hurriedly slipped out of her clothes while Lucas did this.

He turned to see how she was progressing and, as he did so, Autumn reached out with her left hand and guided Lucas in front of her. With her right hand, she carefully slid his erect dick into her mouth.

"Autumn, are you sure this is safe, what would happen if someone came in?" Lucas asked.

She tipped her head back and removed his dick only enough to say, "Can't you see I'm busy? Besides, it isn't polite to talk with your mouth full. Safe? Yes, it's safe; no one has ever gotten pregnant getting her rocks off this way. Now relax."

"Autumn, you're a trip. You know that's not what I meant! And to think I just stopped by to say hello."

"There shouldn't be anyone here for hours. Now relax," murmured Autumn.

Autumn's legs were spread wide apart while seated on the bench, allowing Lucas to stand directly in front of her. She held his dick with her left hand, allowing her to move up and down, almost consuming it entirely while she fondled his balls with her right hand.

"Autumn, you need to stop or I'm going to come."

Removing his dick from her mouth, Autumn looked up and said, "That's the plan." She immediately returned to the task of bringing Lucas to climax.

Lucas's hands rested on her head, following her every movement. His neck craned back and his breathing became heavier and heavier.

"Jeez, Autumn; my dick feels like it's going to explode."

Following that announcement, Autumn turned her focus to the end of his dick, sucking it hard and licking it like a popsicle.

"Autumn, I'm coming."

Those words were music to Autumn's ears. Shifting her attention from the end of his dick, she returned to taking the full length of it deep into her throat, where she could feel Lucas pulsating as he journeyed into ecstasy.

"Autumn, you have to quit—please. I feel like my insides are being shot through the end of my dick. I have to sit down."

"If you really insist."

"I do. Scoot over." As Lucas lowered himself onto the bench, he said, "Autumn, come over here." Then he shifted forward, making room for her to lay down between himself and the wall.

Autumn laid on her back with her legs bent at the knees and her feet flat on the floor. Lucas wasted no time maneuvering himself between her legs, giving him a clear view of that treasure between her legs.

"Autumn, this is my thank you," as he moved his focus from her pubic area to her face.

With that, Lucas slid his hands along the inside of Autumn's legs. He could tell that she was wet, and began to fondle her soft, warm lips with two fingers. Already excited, Autumn began breathing hard and arching her back. Lucas normally began lovemaking with extended foreplay, but excitement caused him to forsake it all and, instead, spread her legs even farther apart, allowing him to lick her passionately.

With exhaustion in her voice, Autumn said, "Lucas, I thought the last time we got together was like dying and going to heaven, but this is delicious. This has to be sinful. I'm going to come."

Hearing that Autumn was nearing climax, Lucas pulled himself up and inserted his dick into Autumn, then began thrusting hard. One second his dick was deep in Autumn, the next it slid nearly all the way out. As Autumn's grip on Lucas's back tightened, his thrusting motion quickened until she grabbed his buttocks and pulled hard, burying his dick inside her and rendering him motionless. As Autumn's climax peaked, Lucas could no longer control himself. He came once again.

Both lay there motionless for a few minutes. Autumn's right arm hung nearly parallel to the floor, with the palm of her hand toward the ceiling. Her right leg, bent at the knee, allowed her right foot to sit flat on the floor. This provided some support as she spread her legs to accommodate Lucas. His weight rested on Autumn's stomach and chest. His left arm hung straight down, toward the floor. His knees rested on the bench, but his calves extended beyond the lip of the cushion.

Together, Lucas and Autumn remained emotionally and physically exhausted, and yet satisfied beyond belief. They were damp with perspiration and just lay there, still held together by Lucas's erect dick, while they regained their strength and composure.

"Lucas, I don't want this moment to end. Can we do it again?"

"That was great. I feel like I could fuck all night, but have you forgotten where we are?"

"Come on, let's do it again."

"Autumn, I would love to, but let's not tempt fate any longer. So far we're safe; let's keep it that way. Why don't you just stay here, clean up, and I'll go next door and do the same? Meet you at the front desk."

"All right, if you must. Let me check and make sure the coast is clear."

Autumn poked her head out the door and looked around. "OK—no one's around. It's safe to go out! See you at the front desk."

After quickly freshening up, Lucas and Autumn met at the front desk and then parted company for the evening.

# CHAPTER THREE
## *Rocky Start*

❧

*S*everal days passed. Lucas arrived at the airport around nine in
the evening, his usual arrival time for a ten-thirty departure.
Heather, the customer service rep on duty, greeted Lucas with an enthusiastic hello.

*Lucas couldn't help but wonder if Autumn had ever talked to Heather
about their rendezvous.*

"Hi! How are you tonight?" Lucas said to her. *She's a beauty,*
he thought, *but I can't be distracted by a pretty woman. Besides, she
and Autumn working in the same office is a recipe for disaster. And
anyway, I don't need or want a relationship with anyone, and if I keep
messing around, that could happen.*

"Heather," he said to her, "you see Mike yet tonight?"

"He passed through a few minutes ago."

"Thanks. He's probably in the office."

As Lucas continued through the lobby, he waved at a couple
of transient pilots waiting on a nearby couch. Curious about a

beautiful Falcon Jet on the ramp, Lucas stopped for some light-hearted pilot conversation.

Lucas asked one of the pilots, "You guys flying the Falcon?"

The other pilot responded with a definitive "Yes," spoken like a proud father.

"It's a beauty. I love the paint job."

"Yeah, we get lots of compliments."

"Who you guys fly for?"

"The plane is owned by Pete Rosco, but today we have his daughter and son-in-law on board. They're at the ballgame. Who do you drive for? And what do you drive?"

"I fly for State Side and tonight I'm flying a Convair 440, but I also fly their King Airs, Lears, and Cessna Jets. A nice job, but I'm scheduled to go to Global shortly. Looks like they're changing my start date, but that has to be worked out."

"Quite a contrast in rides. You know, moving over to a scheduled carrier your life will become one big schedule. What's your name?"

"Lucas. Lucas Sanders."

"My name is Buddy," the first pilot said. "My partner is David. Say hi, David."

"Hi, David," David replied with a smile. "OK; hi, Lucas Sanders. Sorry about that; just couldn't resist."

"How old are you, Mr. Lucas Sanders?" Buddy asked.

"Twenty-nine. Wish I had a dollar for every time someone asked me that question."

"You do look young, but that isn't why I asked. I just wondered how long you've been in this racket. Airline jobs are good, but so is the one you have. Don't be too quick to jump ship."

"I hear ya, but for now I feel compelled to press on. Buddy, David: nice talking with you; I have to finish preparing for tonight's flight. Have a good flight home. Perhaps we'll cross paths again."

"See ya, Lucas. Have a safe flight."

Lucas headed for the office to check in before the routine pre-flight checks to the Convair.

En route to his office, Lucas once again passed directly in front of Heather. This time, he didn't say a word. Heather's demeanor was one of frustration with disappointment written across her face as she reluctantly watched Lucas disappear without saying anything to him.

Upon entering the flight office, Lucas greeted Mike with a big, upbeat "How ya doing tonight, Mike?"

Mike responded in a warm and friendly manner: "Hello, ready for a rough ride tonight?"

"Sure, we can handle it. Because of the weather, I'm going to ask line service to add another hundred gallons of fuel to both sides—just in case."

"Good idea."

"Mike, I'm going to run out and do the preflight and take care of the fuel—anything else you can think I should do? I already filled the thermos with coffee."

"No," Mike said. "Not that I can think of."

Just prior to Lucas leaving the flight office at Gold Coast Aviation to perform the preflight, Mike looked up at Lucas and said, "Heather asked if she could go with us tonight and I told her she could."

Lucas responded abruptly, saying, "Why would you allow that?" *I can't have Autumn and Heather in my world. I will have to be on guard all night.*

"We take guests with us all the time."

"Sure we do, but why Heather?"

"Because she asked if she could go with us tonight. Besides, we both know why she wants to go for a ride. She's wanted to jump your bones for as long as I can remember, and everybody around here knows it. Surely this is no surprise to you, is it?"

"I know, and that's exactly why she shouldn't come with us. Besides, you know we have weather on this trip! Neither of us needs a distraction."

"Come on, Lucas! What's the big deal?"

"I don't have time for romance! I fly all night and go to school all day. Look, I have an airline job waiting for me after school, and I can't screw that up."

"Lucas, have you really looked at this young lady? She is a knockout—she has legs that any guy would love to stroke, the face of a china doll, the innocence of a twelve-year-old looking for her first kiss—there are hundreds of guys in the Midwest who would love to be in your shoes. Besides, what does any of this have to do with Global?"

"First, she isn't a young lady; she's a twenty-one-year-old kid. Secondly—"

"And how old are you, you ungrateful shit?" Mike interrupted. "If you got your dipstick wet a little more often, you wouldn't be so uptight."

"I'm not uptight; I'm busy."

"Too busy for a romp between the sheets with the most beautiful woman you'll ever meet?"

"Fuck you, Mike! I don't care what she has between her legs. I don't have time for that kind of distraction."

"Lucas, will you listen to yourself? Heather is going for a ride with us. No one is asking you to start dating."

Lucas raised his voice: "I understand that, but this is nothing more than a ploy on her part to get something going, and I don't appreciate her abusing you, our friendship, and our willingness to take people for rides."

With that comment, Lucas turned and headed for the office door.

"Lucas," called Mike, "come back here. Does your reaction to Heather have anything to do with the accident?"

Lucas immediately stopped in his tracks. While processing Mike's words, he stared down at the floor. Removing his hand from the doorknob, he turned to partially face Mike. "Maybe," he said. "Have you noticed the similarity between Heather and Morgan too?"

"I have, but I thought that accident was behind you."

"It will never be behind me. I look at Heather, or any attractive girl, and I can still see Morgan lying in the street in a pool of blood. There was nothing I could do for her. Here I am four years later, and I'm still helpless."

"We've talked about this before, Lucas, and you just can't continue blaming yourself for what happened."

"I know that. I do know that, but I can't live through anything like that again. And Heather is so much like Morgan they could be twins. When I see Heather pressing for attention, all I see is Morgan insisting that I take her for a ride on my motorcycle. I see that car pulling out in front of us. I can still hear the tires squealing and the sound of metal as it crumpled beneath me. Here I am with a bright future, and Morgan has never seen another sunrise or sunset. I can't just dismiss that event. It took Morgan's life, and changed me forever."

"Look, Lucas," Mike said. "I can't sit here and tell you to forget what happened. I know that will never happen—but you must not let that accident destroy *two* lives, and I'm afraid that's what's happening. Life isn't fair. For all we know, we may not return from our flight tonight. If we make it back to St. Louis, something could still happen to either of us on our way home. If you're going to do anything, recognize that life is precious and that you should live it to its fullest—appreciate what you have, who you are, your friends, and don't overlook the people who may be a part of your future."

"I know that, Mike, but if I let Heather—or anyone—into my life, I would feel like I was betraying Morgan. That would be more than I could live with."

After saying that, Lucas spent a speechless moment just looking at the floor. Finally, he turned back to Mike and said, "Hey, we need to change the subject. Besides, I need to get some stuff done before we can leave."

"I got ya. Just think about what I said, Lucas."

With those parting words, Lucas opened the door and headed straight to the Convair.

With preflight completed and departure time approaching, Lucas settled into the copilot seat, fastened his belt, and began to arrange his office in the sky. As Lucas finished his cockpit routine, he could hear Mike and Heather enter the plane, followed by Mike raising the stair and locking the door. Mike appeared over Lucas's left shoulder as he entered the cockpit with Heather close behind. Although a tight fit, Lucas didn't even acknowledge Heather's presence.

Lucas had his flying face on, and began to put order to the commotion that took place as Mike and Heather arrived.

"Mike," he said, "we're ready to roll. Heather, if you hang on for just a second I'll get that jump seat set up for you as soon as I get our clearance."

Lucas: "Clearance delivery, this is Convair three-seven-one-three-papa, IFR to Dallas."

Controller: "Convair three-seven-one-three-papa cleared as filed. Departure will be one-one-nine-point-nine—squawk zero-seven-five-eight."

Lucas: "That's Convair thirty-seven-thirteen-papa, cleared as filed— squawk zero-seven-five-eight and departure one-one-nine-point-nine."

Controller: "Read-back correct. Contact ground when ready to taxi."

Lucas: "One-three-papa."

Looking over his left shoulder, Lucas said, "Heather, if you can move up on this ledge, I'll drop the jump seat for you."

As Heather followed his instructions, Lucas's left arm brushed the backs of her legs as he dropped the seat. She was excited knowing that she was going to spend the next five hours just inches from him—the person she'd had a crush on for months.

Seat in place, Heather and Mike buckled their belts and settled in for their departure.

Lucas thought to himself, *This is almost more than I can take. I don't have any interest in entertaining this chick tonight or any night. Although—and I'd never admit this to Mike—she is a looker. Her innocent, young, fresh appearance would qualify her as a spokesperson for the milk industry. Besides, what was she thinking, wearing that loose-fitting miniskirt up here? Therein lies the problem—she wasn't thinking. Screw her. I have one task, and that is to get to Dallas and back home safely.*

"Mike, you ready to go?" Lucas asked aloud.

"Let's do it."

Lucas began reading the checklist to Mike: "OK, starter selector is on the right, door lights out, got the manifold pressure reading. Ramp agent is giving me a thumbs-up on the right—let her crank on the right."

Following that command, Mike engaged the starter on the right engine and the mammoth-sized propeller began to turn. During that phase, Lucas monitored the turning propeller. "There's one blade," he said, "two, three, four, five, six, seven… twelve and ignition."

Shortly after Lucas called for ignition, the engine roared to life, with a heavy cloud of smoke billowing from the exhaust.

"Mike, it's yours for the left side."

After Mike went through a similar routine on the left side, Lucas announced: "Both are fired up and it looks like we're about ready. I'll finish the checklist and we can go. Booster pump and external power is off, cowl flaps open, starter arm normal, door warning lights are out. Checklist completed."

Mike said, in an authoritative voice, "OK, Lucas; let's get this show on the road. Why don't I take the leg to Dallas and you can bring her home?"

"Sounds good," responded Lucas.

Lucas: "Ground control, this is Convair thirty-seven-thirteen-papa, IFR to Dallas at Gold Coast: ready to taxi with information bravo."

The ground controller responded by saying, "Convair three-seven-one-three-papa, taxi to runway three-zero left."

"Roger, three-zero left, one-three-papa," responded Lucas.

The Convair slowly pulled from its parking place and began its journey to runway three-zero left. Once out of the ramp area, the landing lights  were turned off and the plane continued with a slow, lumbering pace between the dimly lit blue taxiway lights.

While Mike and Lucas went through their routine, Heather sat in stunned silence, speechless as she watched two people bring a machine to life. They were about to take her into what appeared to be a boundless night. She now saw Mike and Lucas in a completely different light. She had seen them both as they moved about the lobby area, but never before in such a mesmerizing setting. Watching Mike and Lucas work together was breathtaking—each seemed to know what the other was going to do before he did it.

Now Heather's focus lingered on Lucas, hardly aware that Mike was even present. Heather realized that her feelings for Lucas were about to soar to new levels. It may have been Lucas's mystique that originally captured her interest, but now Heather was about to witness this trim, good-looking guy perform magic as he took her into the waiting night sky.

Despite Lucas being unhappy about Heather joining them, he didn't feel any urge to worry her about the potential rough ride ahead, so he decided to discuss the weather as obscurely as possible while remaining able to navigate through or around the storms.

"So, Mike," he said. "Based on the latest radar summary, do you feel like we may need to go a little south of our course to Tulsa?"

"Looked like it, but you know those cells are likely to move by the time we reach that area."

"You can count on it," responded Lucas. "I saw in the logbook that the radar had been repaired—thank God for that!"

Mike pulled the Convair onto the run-up pad just short of the runway and began the engine run-up phase of the checklist. Lucas, with checklist in hand, began to read and respond to portions of it.

"Fuel, water on, and oil: check; flaps set; generators and inverters: check; radios: check; flight instruments: check; engine instruments—" Lucas glanced at the BMEP instrument and then quickly away.

*Oh my god! What now?* Not wanting to call undue attention to his observation, he forced his eyes back to the checklist. Lucas still couldn't believe his eyes—the jump seat was positioned so that the occupant's legs straddled the rear component of the center console. *I look at the BMEP instrument and I don't see an instrument!* he thought. *Instead, I see the reflection of legs—long, smooth legs—and I can't tell for sure, but I don't think there are panties at the north end of those beautiful legs. I have to spend the next five hours seeing this. Stay focused, stay focused, stay focused! Back to the checklist.*

"Engine instruments: check," he said. "Carb heat: check and cold. Cowl flaps: mid. Ready to roll on my side, Mike! You?"

"Ready. Let's do it," responded Mike.

Lucas changed his radio frequency from ground control to the tower and said, "Tower: Convair three-seven-one-three-papa. The captain says he has his courage up, so we're ready to go on three-zero left."

Controller: "Convair three-seven-one-three-papa: turn left to two-four-zero. Cleared for takeoff."

Lucas: "That's left to two-four-zero, one-three-papa's rolling."

"OK, let's go," said Lucas. "Heather, got your belt on?"

"Sure do!"

"Landing light on," Lucas announced as he reached for one of the many switches on the overhead panel.

Mike told Lucas that the plane was his, and then wiggled the control wheel to avoid any confusion about who was flying the plane.

One-three-papa pulled onto the runway and, with the throttles advanced to takeoff power, all the instruments began to dance in perfect harmony.

During the takeoff roll, Lucas monitored various engine and flight instruments as well as the runway environment. The BMEP instrument was one of those engine instruments that had to be monitored regularly during this phase of flight. Although Lucas's attention moved between many instruments and tasks during this phase of takeoff, he couldn't help but hesitate when he noticed his perfect view up Heather's skirt. The obscure lighting was the only thing preventing him from confirming whether or not she had panties on. Even so, he could feel his dick respond as his imagination toyed with the uncertainty.

As the plane rapidly accelerated, Heather thought to herself that she had never seen anything like this. So much was going on that it took the attention of two people, and yet it appeared effortless to the casual passenger. She wondered how she could ever repay Mike for allowing her to make this trip. The only thing, she thought, that would make it even better would be getting a little attention from Lucas. She decided to try and be content with herself occupying a small piece of his world.

The control tower operator said, "Convair three-seven-one-three-papa: contact departure on one-one-nine-point-nine. Have a nice flight."

Lucas responded, "Roger, one-three-papa. You have a good one, too. Departure control, this is three-seven-one-three-papa with ya, climbing through two thousand."

"Three-seven-one-three-papa, this is departure. Proceed on course."

"One-three-papa. Mike, I'm going to work with the radar and see if I can't get a better feel for where we're going to encounter those thunderstorms."

Lucas knew that if he could focus on one thing—like the radar—he was much less likely to try to figure out whether or not Heather was wearing panties.

*This is exactly why I don't need these kinds of distractions in my life*, Lucas thought. *We have weather to deal with, and I'm sitting here getting a boner just thinking about some gal and what she may not be wearing. Come to think of it, Autumn didn't have panties on the last time we did the deed; I'm betting Heather doesn't either. No panties— maybe I don't understand what customer service reps do. Anyway, there will be plenty of time for the ladies when I get out of school and get on with Global.*

Lucas always scanned the engine instruments along with the flight instruments, even if he wasn't flying the plane. Every time his scan included the BMEP, there Heather was in all her glory, exposed to the world from the waist down. Her dark, obscure reflection stimulated Lucas's curiosity—as well as other things. *I can't help but wonder what is being concealed by the darkness,* he thought.

While Lucas tried to get a good fix on the weather, Mike focused on flying the plane, with an occasional lapse into a trance-like state as he reflected on other events in his life. When this happened, Mike was oblivious to anything going on around him. Such behavior was typical for Mike, and Lucas knew about his tendency to allow his mind to wander. Lucas believed that Mike's short attention span was, at its core, due to the drinking problem that he'd had for years.

The flight continued to go smoothly, and Heather enjoyed her new experience. Flying was not new to her, but she'd never before realized that so much went on at the head of the plane. The busy cockpit almost overstimulated her senses—there were so many instruments, knobs, and switches. It was hard for her to imagine how anyone could keep up with so much at one time.

The instrument panel exuded a warm, red glow, so nothing in the cockpit kept its real color—everything and everyone adopted a very seductive glow.

Lucas busily adjusted the radar to get a good feel for the line of thunderstorms ahead. They would either need to pick their way through them, or fly around them; that decision would in large part be determined by what he saw, he knew. Thunderstorms are very dynamic, and radar summaries obtained prior to departure don't remain accurate for very long.

Though trying to focus on this single task, Lucas couldn't help noticing Heather's presence. *She sure is warm,* he thought to himself. *Her right leg is all but rubbing my left arm. It's like every hair on my arm has become a nerve linked directly to my dick. Even the hair on my arm is getting stiff. I don't even know whether I'm brushing her leg, or just think I am. I would never admit this to Mike, but having her on board is sort of nice. It's a lot nicer having her on board than some of the guys we fly.*

*I have to focus on the radar, but I can't help but wonder if she is wearing panties. Get a grip! I'm paying way too much attention to the reflection of Heather and those beautiful, long, gorgeous legs that I'd love to explore. Bet I would find out about her panties then! Panties—what is happening to me? I'm obsessing! Radar, radar, radar.*

The radar looked bright and full of color, lit up like a Christmas tree. Anyone with any experience seeing thunderstorm activity—even on TV—would characterize it as being ominous. Lucas decided that he had to give Heather an update.

He turned to look over his left shoulder so he could look Heather in the eyes. As they made eye contact, he saw a beautiful young girl with the face of an angel, her eyes dark and inviting. Shifting in his seat, he could see her more clearly— straddling the console with her miniskirt as high as could be. Conscious of how exposed she was, he had to be very careful not to break eye contact and explore her lovely, soft body, and especially the place where her legs came together.

"Heather," Lucas said, "we have some weather we're going have to go through, so it might get a little rough. I want you to pull your belt tight and hang on. We're going to be busy, so we won't be able to talk to you. Don't worry; we do this stuff all the time."

Having briefed Heather, Lucas swung back around and tightened his own belt. He then turned to Mike to share his thoughts about the approaching weather.

"Mike, we have about twenty-five more miles of good weather, with about fifty miles of thunderstorm activity we'll have to pick our way through. Mike, did you hear me? *Mike*, goddamn it, are you sleeping? MIKE, wake your ass up! You're supposed to be flying this plane!"

As Mike jerked his head up, he turned to Lucas and said, "Bullshit! The autopilot is flying it, and I might say it is doing a better job than you would."

"Mike, we've been through this before. Were you drinking before we left?"

"None of your fucking business."

"Bullshit! It *is* my business. It is going to take both of us to get through this weather, and we can't do it if you're drunk! Why do I put up with this shit night after fucking night? Heather, relax. Like the weather, we go through this shit all the time, too."

"Lucas," Mike snapped. "Shut the fuck up and tell me what you found on the radar."

Though still pissed, Lucas knew that the miles were being eaten up quickly and this wasn't the time to argue.

"The first thing I want to do is to get a release from Center so we can do our own thing. If it's OK with you, why don't I fly the plane and you fly the engines? Having studied the radar, I have a good feel for how we can get through this stuff."

"Fine by me—let me know when you want it," responded Mike.

Lucas began the process of getting a change in their flight plan: "Kansas City Center, this is Convair three-seven-one-three-papa."

"One-three-papa, this is Kansas City Center. Go ahead."

"Kansas City Center, one-three-papa would like to deviate from our flight plan as necessary, to pick our way through this line of thunderstorms."

"One-three-papa, that's approved. There are no other planes in the area. Just give us a call when you want to rejoin the airway, and if you would, give us an update on the weather when you have a chance."

"Roger, one-three-papa."

Lucas dropped both of his seat's armrests. With both hands on the wheel and both arms resting on the armrests for stability, Lucas said, "OK, Mike; I have the plane."

"The plane is yours, Lucas. I have the engines."

By that time, they began to experience a light chop, signaling a pending change in weather. Having been through this many times before, Lucas and Mike knew what to expect.

"Mike, see this patch of light green?" Lucas pointed to the radar screen. "This is where I'm headed. After about five miles, I'm going to make a twenty-degree left turn to keep us out of the heavy stuff, and I think we will be able to shift back to the right after about twenty miles, but we'll have to play that by ear."

The plane began to pick up more turbulence, and light rain beaded on the windshield.

Heather became very much aware that Lucas and Mike had stopped arguing, and that they had both adopted a serious tone and a single focus. She also realized that her romantic mood and environment had suddenly changed to one of at least mild concern. Seeing lightning directly ahead and rain on the windshield was a new experience for her. The rain caused the cabin's noise level to increase significantly. Heather tried to sort out what was happening, and to also compare each sound and sight with something more familiar.

The rain grew heavier and louder.

The sound of the rain was very much like a million BBs striking the windshield at one time. Seeing lightning from a pilot's view is another foreign sight hard to describe but it looked to Heather that the whole sky was lighting up.

Shortly after a bright flash, Lucas turned to Heather and shouted above the noise of the rain, "That's the stuff we need to avoid!

It's about ten miles ahead of us." To Mike, he announced, "I'm going to make that right turn now."

The plane shook violently, gaining and losing hundreds of feet in altitude every few seconds.

"Mike, watch those engines!" Lucas yelled above the noise of rain beating against the windshield. "I'm going to try to keep the wings level. I can't even keep a steady heading. Mike, why don't you pull the power back? See if slowing down will help."

"Good idea—don't want the manifold pressure to jump up on us, and a little less airspeed may give our passenger a better ride," Mike said, turning to smile at Heather.

Heather felt her anxiety worsening. When she'd asked Mike if she could go along on their trip, a near-death experience hadn't been what she'd had in mind. Being in the middle of a thunderstorm wasn't anything like being at home snuggled up on the couch with a special guy, listening to the rain and thunder. *This is the roughest ride I have experienced anywhere*, she thought to herself. *I can't even think of anything to compare it to. I can't see the lightning; instead, the whole outside world simply lights up. I don't hear the thunder and have no idea how close the lightning is. And Lucas said they do this all the time. I think I'd find a new job.*

"Mike, see the light green on the radar?" Lucas tried pointing to the radar screen, but quickly returned both hands to the control wheel.

Heather wondered whether Lucas held onto the wheel to keep his body from bouncing around, or whether it was instead necessary to fly the plane.

"I think we can squeeze through that opening. What do you think, Mike?"

"Looks good to me, Lucas—that should also put us on the back side of this front."

Heather had forgotten the warm feelings in her stomach caused by Lucas's arm brushing up against her leg. That romantic encounter had been replaced with uncertainty and a little fear. For the last twenty minutes, her leg had been slapping against Lucas's elbow and there hadn't been anything romantic or seductive about it. Perched on the jump seat, there wasn't anything of substance for her to hold onto. She thought to herself, *If it weren't for this seat belt, I would've been making love to the center console long ago.* Her posture, legs spread apart to straddle the console, had seemed so seductive when the flight got underway, but had since become uncomfortable, to say the least.

The Convair reached the other side of the front, and the turbulence disappeared as quickly as it had started.

Lucas turned to look partly over his shoulder and said, "You can relax now, Heather." He lifted the armrests that he had been using to stabilize his arms.

Beyond the windshield, they could see stars in the sky and lights on the ground. The noise had disappeared, as had the turbulence.

"Mike, you want the plane back?" asked Lucas.

"No, just keep it—I'm going to give Center an update on the weather."

Mike called Oklahoma Center and said, "Oak Center, this is Convair thirty-seven-thirteen-papa."

"Go ahead, thirty-seven-thirteen-papa."

"One-three-papa has cleared the weather and would advise other planes in the area that we encountered moderate turbulence and heavy rain as we picked our way through the front just north of Springfield. We're going to proceed direct to Dallas at eight thousand."

"Got it, one-three-papa—appreciate the update. Are you making a return trip tonight?"

"Sure are," responds Mike.

"Your trip home should be uneventful—looks like that system you just came through is falling apart."

"Thanks; wasn't looking forward to doing it again—couldn't sleep!"

"OK," the controller said, laughing.

The cockpit got very quiet, with everyone engrossed in their own thoughts, appreciating a tranquil flight once again. The remainder of the trip was uneventful, including the turnaround in Dallas.

On the way back to St. Louis, everyone remained silent. It was late, and there wasn't anything taking place to encourage discussion. Mike flew the plane while Lucas focused on first-officer duties. Heather napped most of the way home. She leaned far to the right in order to use the bulkhead as a headrest. It wasn't particularly comfortable, but the hum of the engines was soothing.

# CHAPTER FOUR
## *Reliving the Present*

Despite sleeping most of the way back to St. Louis, Heather occasionally woke to thoughts of Lucas, causing her to reflect on what it took just to be in the jump seat of that plane, occupying a small piece of his world.

Heather had been fascinated by Lucas from the day she began working for Gold Coast Aviation as a customer service rep; as she saw it, her job title was nothing more than a fancy phrase for "receptionist."

Like most pilots, Lucas only came around shortly before a flight, so Heather never really had an opportunity to meet him. She wondered how a person she didn't even know could capture her attention so fully. What did he have that made her become so self-conscious when he was around? It couldn't merely be his uniform, because many others wore uniforms. She decided that it must be a simple physical attraction, but felt confident there was more to be discovered.

Heather's work area wasn't fancy or inviting for customers. The lobby area had a high ceiling with long fluorescent lights. The lights weren't even recessed, but instead hung directly from the ceiling. The floor was a gray tile beginning to show wear. There were several chairs and a couch around the outside wall, but they, too, showed wear. They were really only there for transient pilots, so management didn't find it necessary to spend money on quality materials. The walls had a few photographs of airplanes, but all of them were old and in need of dusting.

The lobby doors opened on the airport side of the building—the ramp, and in the back of the lobby a door opened into the hangar. A third door opened to the parking lot, and was referred to as the front, or "main," door. When any two doors were opened at the same time, the lobby became like a wind tunnel, very cold in the winter and very hot in the summer. The receptionist's desk was located behind a modest counter, and only displayed a few necessary pilot supplies. It also came with a small space heater and a fan, tools to deal with the extreme temperature fluctuations. In the summer, reps usually only wore enough to keep them modest. Such an arrangement became popular with the pilots, possibly ensuring that the situation would never be remedied.

Heather could clearly remember the first time she'd ever seen Lucas. He'd passed through the lobby, obviously on a mission. He stared directly ahead, looking so serious. He didn't even notice Heather, and yet it seemed to her that she wasn't seeing the *real* Lucas. She had no specific reason to think that; it was just a hunch. Later she found out that he'd had equipment problems that day—problems that needed immediate attention in order to deliver his cargo on time.

As Heather continued to reflect on the night that Lucas came into her life, she couldn't help but wonder what life would have been like had she finished college. Working the second shift at a fixed-base operation wasn't exactly what she thought life would be like at twenty-one. The working conditions weren't very good and neither was the pay, although it did pay enough for her to afford a one-bedroom furnished apartment just six miles from the airport.

Many pilots passed through the lobby every night, and each added a little spice to what would otherwise be a humdrum job. Hardly a night passed without some hotshot pilot putting the make on her. Although not a particularly outgoing person, Heather didn't mind the attention and realized that most of the flirting was nothing more than a guy's attempt to relive his youth or pass the time while his plane was being serviced.

Evenings usually passed quickly, in part because of the traffic. There would generally be fifteen to twenty freighters passing through the operation a night, either taking a load somewhere or bringing one to St. Louis. With fifteen to twenty planes would come between thirty and forty pilots, each of whom often needed as much attention as his plane.

When asked, Heather described herself as an average gal who could be found in any mall on a Saturday night. She was also willing to admit that she probably received more compliments than the average person. She had even been encouraged to run for Miss Missouri by her friends, but decided she didn't want the attention. Besides, most contestants were tall with long legs; she wasn't convinced that a five-foot-six, 115-pound brunette would have a chance of winning.

She found her way into the jump seat on a bumpy trip to Dallas because of Lucas. She wished that he would spend more time in the lobby. If he did, she knew that she might be able to strike up a conversation and find out a little more about her mystery heartthrob. Since that was unlikely, she felt compelled to figure out another way to spend more time in his presence.

She'd pondered this question for a long time, and her creativity and persistence eventually led to success. She knew that State Side pilots often took passengers for the fun of it, or helped pilots get home after their flights. Lucas's flights usually departed shortly after Heather's shift was up, so she knew she had a workable plan. Since she knew that Mike and Lucas always flew together, she decided to ask Mike for a ride. That's all she needed—one flight. She hoped it would lead to another as she tried to find a way into Lucas's life.

"Heather, make sure your belt is tight; we'll be landing shortly," announced Lucas.

Only semiconscious, Heather heard Lucas's voice and jerked back to reality.

"I got it, thanks," she said. "Jeez, I must have slept most of the way home. Did I miss anything?"

"Not a thing."

# CHAPTER FIVE

## Dreams Come True

❧

A few days later, and still determined to spend more time with Lucas, Heather stopped Mike on his way through the lobby. "OK if I go with you guys again tonight?" she asked.

"Once wasn't enough for ya, huh?"

"It was fun! Besides, I have this thing for Lucas and he doesn't even know I exist. I hoped that after the last trip, he might ask me out."

"Sure. No one else is going tonight. It will be a quickie, though. We're just going to Omaha tonight."

"That's OK. I just want Lucas to know who I am."

"Well, little lady, a cockpit isn't the place to get to know someone. Our cockpit is our office—our workplace."

"I know, and I won't bother either of you—I was OK last time, wasn't I?"

"Sure you were. I'm just saying that it'll be difficult for Lucas to get to know you on these trips."

"I know, but I don't know of any other way to be close to him or spend time with him."

"Not a problem. We should be departing around ten thirty. Oh, and when you see Lucas, will you mention that I'm looking for him?"

"Sure will, and thanks."

Mike walked off, proud of his little scheme to have Heather deliver a message for him. He'd be the first to admit that he wasn't a matchmaker, but Heather was a cute girl, and if he could help move romance in her direction—well, why not?

Shortly after Mike walked away, Lucas came strolling through the lobby, en route to the office. As he walked past the counter, Heather sprung to her feet with the enthusiasm of a lottery winner, shouting, "Lucas, Lucas, just a second!"

Hearing urgency in Heather's voice, Lucas nearly stopped dead in his tracks.

"Mike wanted me to be sure to mention that he was looking for you," said Heather. "I think he's in the office."

"Oh, OK. Did he tell you what he wanted?"

"No, but he said I can ride with you guys to Omaha tonight. I hope that's OK with you."

"Sure. OK by Mike, OK by me. See you shortly. Incidentally, how is Autumn doing?"

"I saw her last night just before I got off work, but we didn't really talk. Why do you ask?"

"Just curious. I saw her the night of the storm and she seemed rather frazzled. When you see her, tell her I said 'hi.'"

"I'll see her shortly and I'll mention that you were asking about her." *There is no way I am going to relay that message to Autumn. I'm not stupid! Autumn is a looker. Girls like her are a nightmare for people like me. She has boobs to die for. She has a way of talking to guys that always gets her asked out. I'm confused. Lucas has never asked about her before. In my last conversation with Autumn, she said she wasn't dating anyone, and she didn't express interest in Lucas or anyone else. This is definitely going to require further investigation. I can't get Lucas to notice me, and here he is asking me about another girl—and a gorgeous one, at that.*

Lucas opened the office door, stuck his head in, and asked Mike what he wanted.

"Lucas, I did ask for you, but can't remember what I wanted. If I think of it, I'll be sure to tell you."

"Hey, I got this call from Global and they're asking for another interview. It's about delaying my start date. If you recall I mentioned this to you earlier."

"Again, why are they delaying your start date?"

"Has something to do with hiring experienced pilots, furloughed from other airlines. They're running out of seats in my class—I think the fellow I'm talking with said they were down to two seats, but they'll probably hold those for more experienced pilots."

"Experience always gets in the way of young pilots."

"I guess," said Lucas, concerned. "I asked if there was anything I could do to move things along, to keep my start date the same, and he said they'll schedule another interview for me. Think I have anything to worry about?"

"Probably not, but like I said before: experience is always a killer for young pilots. I'm sure they don't have any doubts about you; they just want to hire as much experience as they can."

"Mike, you've been in this business for a long time. What do you think?"

"Look, whether you get the Global job or not, you have a good job here. Being a corporate pilot has a lot to offer."

"I know," said Lucas. "But I've dreamed of an airline job since I was twelve. I can remember as a kid, when my mother worked for Great Western; I would fly free all over the country just to fly. I took a plane to New York and back the same day just for the experience. That was when kids could still visit the pilots in the cockpit. I would go up front and be in heaven. I idolized those pilots."

"Too bad about Great Western going out of business; seems to be the trend in the airline industry. As for Global, don't let any of this get you down. Did they pull the offer?"

"No."

"Then what are you fretting about?"

"All right. Did you remember what you wanted me for?"

"Don't have a clue."

"That's cool. I'm going to do the preflight." Lucas began to walk away, but hesitated and turned back toward Mike to say, "What's with Heather? She said she was going with us again tonight."

"She asked if she could go, and I didn't see any reason to say no."

Lucas restated his previous concern: "You know, Mike, she has me in the crosshairs of Cupid's bow. It's like I have a target painted on my back."

Mike responded sharply, saying, "Lucas, we've been through this before. You run your life as you see fit. I'm not going to interfere with it, but you shouldn't be so uptight about this Heather thing."

"That's just it. I don't have a 'Heather thing' and don't want a 'Heather thing.'"

"You didn't have a problem last time, did you? Besides, she is a beautiful young girl—a nice person who happens to work for Gold Coast, and we always take their employees for a ride. How could I say no to her?"

"OK. I'm just beginning to feel pressure from someone."

"Lucas, how old are you?"

"Twenty-nine."

"I don't want to sound like your dad, but if you slept with the ladies a little more often, you wouldn't be so uptight."

"Mike, sex isn't a cure-all."

"If you tried it more often, you wouldn't say that. Besides, how do you think I stay in such good shape?"

"If you're an example of what sex will do for a person, then I wouldn't go around promoting it like you just discovered a new wonder drug."

"What the fuck does that mean?"

"Just that you're no poster child for what romance will do for a person. You know that she reminds me of Morgan. I don't want to talk about this anymore. See you in a few minutes." Lucas closed the door with purpose.

Lucas proceeded to the Convair and performed his usual pre-flight. Unlike most nights, he decided to stay with the plane while workers loaded in the cargo. Meanwhile, Heather clocked out, consciously deciding not to say anything to Autumn. Instead, she dashed straight to the office, where Mike was completing some paperwork. Not wanting to interfere with Mike, she slipped in and took a seat at one end of the desk.

When Mike finished his last entry, he tilted his head toward Heather, his eyes still scanning his paperwork and said, "You know that Lucas is going to be a project, right?"

"What do you mean?" asked Heather.

"At the moment, he has his mind on one thing—that airline job waiting for him when he graduates. Women and relationships are not high on his list of priorities. If you want to get his attention, you'll have to be persistent. You are always welcome to go with us if we have room. Incidentally, you don't need to mention that we had this conversation. He already suspects a conspiracy of some sort."

"I'm glad you told me this. Do I have any chance with him?"

"I think you have a good chance with him. He doesn't have a girlfriend—at least not one that I know about—and he pretty much sticks to himself." Mike looked up at Heather and caught her eye. "Now I'm going to tell you something that *must* stay between us. Lucas has a demon from the past. He lost a previous girlfriend. I mean she died. Just be sensitive of that. He may take a little more encouragement than other fellows you've dated. At the end of the day, though, you are a gorgeous young lady and he would be a fool not to chase you around town."

"Nice of you to say that. I hope things work out between us, and I promise I won't say a word to him."

"I do, too. Be patient."

The word "too" from Mike's mouth was still in the air when Lucas stuck his head through the door to announce that the Convair was ready to go and he had their clearance in hand. After making his announcement, Lucas withdrew from the doorway and returned to the plane.

With a slight grin, Mike gave Heather a quick wink and said, "Let's hit it."

Mike and Heather ascended the stairs to the plane. The cabin's entrance was just outside the cockpit. Once inside the plane, a sharp left turn and a few steps took Mike and Heather into the cockpit area. The passage to the flight deck was narrow and about six feet long. The flight deck was elevated about a foot above the floor. On the left side of the aisle was a floor-to-ceiling stack of radios. On the right side was a small access door intended to be used by ground support personnel. Two people could just squeeze past one another if both of them were small.

Heather stood at the door leading to the cockpit. When she peered in, she could see Lucas seated to the right. From just a few feet away, she watched him prepare for their flight.

Mike brought up the stairs and secured the door. After confirming that the door was locked, he moved with purpose to the left seat, clearing the aisle so that Heather could approach the deck. Wanting to go mostly unnoticed, she just stood there, watching as Mike and Lucas converted their mass of metal into a creation with a life of its own. She couldn't help but think of the cylindrical chamber as some sort of a wondrous, mechanical Frankenstein.

Once Mike and Lucas got underway, Lucas asked Heather to step onto the flight deck so he could lower and latch the jump seat. Having done this once before, she no longer felt like a rookie, and instead stepped up with confidence and stood close to Lucas, turned so that her back was mostly to him. This allowed Lucas to reach behind her and drop the jump seat into position. Lucas had chosen his short-sleeved uniform for the night's flight, and his innocent decision, made hours ago, contributed to Heather's sexual frustration. The small cockpit meant that clearing enough space for Lucas to reach the jump seat required an almost acrobatic maneuver.

When Lucas reached behind Heather, his bare arm rubbed the back of her right thigh. As he continued trying to release the stubborn latch, his rustling put serious pressure on her leg, even lifting her miniskirt as he brushed against the cheeks of her ass. His skin against her legs, and then her ass, sent a chill up Heather's spine and caused her senses to come suddenly to life.

"Mike, remind me to report that fucking latch when we get back," Lucas said as he finished. "Sorry about the language, Heather; I nearly sprain my wrist every time I mess with it."

"That's OK—not like I've never heard it before."

With seat and Heather in place, Lucas shifts his focus back to business, trying to forget that his arm was just under the dress of a beautiful young lady. If the latch hadn't been so difficult to wrangle, he may have even enjoyed the touch of her warm, soft leg. In a different setting, in fact, he would have felt guilty for feeling up a woman he hardly knew.

Lucas turned and looked at Heather and at the legs he just fondled. Then he looks at Heather's face and sees her watching him. Suddenly feeling self-conscious, Lucas turned away and pulled the checklist from the sunshield.

"Lucas, are you finished screwing around over there?" asked Mike. "Are you going to make this short trip an all-night endeavor? Fuck!"

"What got your panties in a wad?" asked Lucas.

"Can we just get this show on the road?"

"Sure. Let's do it."

"Lucas, Heather," Mike said more calmly, "sorry about my little outburst."

"Not a problem, Mike. I'm with you. Let's go," said Lucas with enthusiasm.

"Guys, do your own thing," said Heather. "I certainly don't want my presence to get in the way."

Lucas began to wonder what else the night had in store for him. It only took a few seconds to make that discovery. As he scanned the instrument panel, Lucas found that he could once again see up Heather's skirt in the BMEP instrument's reflection. *My God!* Lucas thought to himself. *Here is a lady that I have no interest in, and yet I've already had my hand up her skirt and may as well be able to see her business. I am a living, breathing guy—how can I focus on my job when I have her hooch staring at me? We have to get this plane to Omaha and back, and I'm sitting here getting a woody. I'm supposed to be sitting here thinking about takeoff speeds and stuff like that. Instead I'm thinking about getting into some girl's pants, if she has any on. This was never discussed in flight school.*

Despite Lucas's distraction, the trio had an uneventful trip to Omaha and everyone arrived in a good mood. Their flight back to St. Louis also started off well.

As they approached St. Louis, Heather began to frantically wonder what she would have to do to get Lucas to pay attention to her. He'd been nice to her, but he was nice to everybody. She racked her brain to figure out a way to get him to see her differently. The closer they got to St. Louis, the more her anxiety grew, until she had a hard time thinking rationally.

*Maybe I should stop beating around the bush and just throw myself at him.* Reality set in. *That won't work. That will just drive him away. No, if we get together it will have to be his idea.*

As they began their final approach, it came to her. She thought to herself, *I'll invite everyone over to my place for a nightcap.* Although no one else could tell, a celebration began to take place in Heather's heart and mind. She became convinced that her idea would move forward her relationship with Lucas. *He might see me differently if we can spend some quality time together—away from airplanes and on my turf.*

As the trio descended the airplane's stairs, Heather took the lead. Just before reaching the ramp, she stopped and spun to her right, so she could see both Lucas and Mike. Trying to make it sound like an afterthought, Heather said, "This was a quick trip. Why don't you guys come over to my place for a night-cap?"

Mike responded first, saying, "I'd love to. Lucas, you in?"

"I could swing by for a little while. I have class at ten later this morning, so I can't stay long—gotta get some sleep, you know!"

Unlike most evenings, the route to their cars took them through the lobby rather than asking Heather to weave around the airplanes parked in the hanger. As they entered the lobby, Autumn greeted them warmly: "Welcome back to St. Louis. So how was your trip tonight? Better than the last one?"

Heather was quick to answer. "Much better than the last. Tonight was perfect."

"You guys look like you're on a mission!" Autumn said. "You aren't just going to pass through and leave, are you? Anybody want to stick around and chat? It's been dead all night."

Mike, Lucas, and Heather all stood directly across the counter from Autumn. Each glanced at the other, not sure how to respond to Autumn's invitation.

"Hey, Autumn," Lucas finally said.

Not wanting the conversation between Autumn and Lucas to go any further, Heather interrupted, saying, "Autumn, these guys have put up with me for a couple of flights. I figure the least I can do is have them over for a nightcap."

"Sounds like fun. If you wait until six, I'll go with you."

"That offer's hard to refuse," said Heather, "but Lucas can only stay for a little while."

"Likely story. You two need a chaperone."

"I don't think a chaperone is needed," retorted Heather, "but if so, we have Mike."

Mike quickly responded by saying, "Hey, that makes me feel like a third wheel. What's this chaperone stuff? You don't think I need watching?"

"Mike, I'm just joking," said Heather.

"I know," said Mike.

Heather turned to face Autumn and said, "Thanks for the offer, Autumn, but not tonight. See you tomorrow night."

Autumn responded with an upbeat voice. "You guys take care and have fun! See you tomorrow."

On the surface, everyone seemed to be having a good time as they matched wits with one another, while Lucas felt out of place. Nothing being said sounded cute or funny. Given the choice, he'd rather stick around and talk to Autumn instead of going for a drink with Mike and Heather. Heather was feeling anxious, and Autumn was annoyed by being excluded from their outing. Mike was just busy trying to think of a way to get things moving for Heather.

As the three reached the Gold Coast exit, Mike started to open the door for the others, but then turned to Lucas and Heather. "I just remembered that I have a meeting at eight tomorrow," he said. "I've got to get some shut-eye. Have a good night, though, you two."

"Join us next time?" Heather asked before Lucas even had time to register Mike's excuse.

*How did I let this happen?* Lucas thought to himself. *There won't be a "next time."*

The three passed through the lobby and into the parking lot.

Mike turned back to Heather and Lucas on his way to his own car. "Have a nice evening! See ya tomorrow night," he said. Lucas and Heather walked to their own cars, which were separated by a few hundred feet. The lot was almost empty, so they had no trouble keeping an eye on one another. Heather pulled out first, followed by Lucas.

Lucas had never seen any personal aspect of Heather except for her warm, soft legs extending beyond the bounds of her miniskirt. Behind the wheel, he thought to himself, *This is strange. Here I am just watching Heather pull out in her car, and I suddenly feel a personal connection with her. I've had her legs brush against me—no,* rub *against me. I've looked up her skirt—well, that's not exactly how it went, but I may as well have. Every time I looked at the BMEP instrument, that's all I could see. Why does seeing her pull out in her dark burgundy Mustang feel like a personal connection? My God, how am I going to feel if I look inside her refrigerator? Maybe I should just drive off.* As he continued to think about the next few hours, he began to feel nervous, uncomfortable, and out of control—not a good feeling for anyone, especially a pilot.

Just ahead of Lucas, Heather could see his headlights following her every turn, as though they were connected—as though she suddenly had control over a piece of the evening. *Could this actually be happening?* she wondered. *Is Lucas actually following me home? I owe Mike for this one!*

Heather made the final turn into her parking lot. Lucas was still close behind. Her parking spot was right next to her back door, which opened onto a small patio. Lucas pulled in next to her, to park in the slot marked "Guest."

They both left their cars at about the same time. With two quick, electric chirps, both locked their doors. Lucas wasn't sure why he locked his car, but wrote it off to habit. He had no intention of spending any time with Heather.

He followed Heather onto the patio without speaking, and then through the door into her apartment.

"Have a seat, Lucas." Heather gestured at the oversized love seat. "I'm going to go get comfortable—I'll be right back to make you something to drink."

Heather disappeared into her bedroom, but left the door cracked in case she wanted to say something to Lucas. Out of sight, she pondered what to do next. Getting comfortable was nothing more than an excuse to buy a little time to sort things out. *I can't just seduce him. Whatever happens tonight must be Lucas's idea, or I'll never have a second chance. I'm so excited I can hardly contain myself. I can almost feel him between my legs. Control yourself, Heather, or there won't be a tomorrow!* Out of ideas, Heather decided to put her running clothes on. They were stylish, but no one could accuse her of seducing anyone in those clothes. Pulling her pants up was like putting on a second coat of skin, which excited her groin even more. *What now? This won't work. I can't be this excited and still let Lucas take the lead.*

She yelled through the opened door, "Lucas, I'll be right there! Be patient!"

She pulled her pants off and tossed them into the corner. *Now what? What's wrong with this picture? I'm in my bedroom, bare-ass naked, and the guy I want to jump is in my living room completely dressed.* Rummaging through her dirty clothes, she came across a pair of running shorts and decided they'd be OK for the night. In the same basket, she found a discarded shirt inherited from her dad. It was much too big, but it was comfortable. In fact, the shirt extended beyond her shorts, which gave the illusion of being without any pants. She wondered whether her thrown-together outfit was too suggestive, but quickly dismissed the thought in favor of toying with Lucas's manly urges.

Emerging from the bedroom, Heather headed directly to the kitchen area. She had to walk right in front of Lucas to get there.

"Hey," he said, acknowledging Heather as she headed to the kitchen. Seeing Heather in a shirt large enough to be a night shirt was a bit concerning following her announcement about getting comfortable. Once again, Lucas found himself wondering what she may or may not have on underneath.

The kitchen was small and blended in with the living room, the two separated only by a breakfast bar. There was a narrow aisle between the bar and kitchen cabinets and sink. The refrigerator was located on the end wall. From the kitchen, Heather could see Lucas fidgeting, flipping through a *People* magazine that she'd left on the couch.

"Lucas, what would you like to drink? I have Bud Select, a little white wine, a bottle of red wine, iced tea, and Dr. Pepper—or I could make coffee. You pick."

Lucas looked thoughtful before he said, "I'll have a DP."

"You got it. One DP is headed your way."

Heather poured herself a glass of red wine and emptied a can of Dr. Pepper into a glass filled with ice.

With wine in her left hand and Dr. Pepper in her right, she joined Lucas on the love seat. She handed Lucas his drink and then put a coaster on the coffee table within his reach. Heather positioned herself at the other end of her oversized love seat and sat facing Lucas. She pulled her knees under her chin and balanced her wineglass between them, using her hands to steady it. Her bare feet almost touched Lucas's thighs.

Just sitting on the same couch, so close to Lucas, made all logic disappear from Heather's otherwise controlled mind. She'd gotten excited in the bedroom, and could feel the same warm glow overtaking her desire to remain calm and let Lucas take the lead.

Heather found herself at a loss for words. She wondered how to make idle conversation with someone she didn't even know, yet had such strong feelings for.

"So, Lucas," she said, "tell me about yourself. I see you at the airport and have been fortunate enough to fly with you a couple of times, but I don't know anything about you."

"That's pretty much it," Lucas said. "I go to school during the day and fly at night."

While he talked, Lucas thought to himself, *This is painful! Who gives a shit what I do?* At the same time, he realized that perhaps the most beautiful lady he'd ever met was sitting on the couch across from him. *If I allowed myself to,* he thought, *I could get a hard-on just looking at her.* This reminded Lucas of the "fight or flee" concept that he'd learned about in school. *Do I take the easy way out and flee, or do I fight all of my internal instincts and get to know Heather?*

"What about you?" he finally asked her. "You work the evening shift at Gold Coast—what else do you do?"

"Generally sleep late, read—and I really enjoy exercising. Mostly running. I like to cook. It's my way of being creative."

"Are you good?"

"Everyone I've cooked for seems to like it."

"Interesting!"

Lucas had never considered small talk his forte, and still couldn't wait for the opportunity to bail. On the other hand, most pilots he knew were a little curious and open to adventure—risk had to be held to a minimum as a pilot, but exploration was generally OK. *I probably fit that profile as well*, he thought. His internal conflict continued to build, since she *was* beautiful and sexy. Just sitting there, crunched up on the couch, she looked so cute. His dick started to get hard as he wondered what it would be like to slip it between her legs.

A thought suddenly hit him, like a tornado swirling through his mind. If he didn't relax a little, he might never know what he was be missing. *Wow! Am I really interested in learning more about this gal, or do I just want to screw her? Damn it, I hate this relationship-building shit. Autumn made it easy; a quick fuck and it was over.*

Heather could sense Lucas's uneasiness, and tried to relieve him from having to create small talk. She knew that all pilots had one thing in common: an endless supply of war stories. She also knew that the easiest way to engage a pilot in conversation was to get him started telling stories.

"Lucas, what's the most exciting thing that's ever happened to you in an airplane?"

With a reflective, puzzled look on his face, Lucas turned to his left, so that he could look at Heather head-on. He turned back, as though staring into space, and looked at Heather once more. Giving Heather an answer required him to reflect on the previous several years. He suddenly felt relaxed, an unusual calmness that passed over him like the eye of a hurricane.

"Hard to say; every flight is an adventure. That's what I like about flying. Some adventures are more memorable than others, of course." For whatever reason, just talking about flying makes this situation feel so much more familiar. "Two flights come to mind, although if we had the time and you had the interest, I could probably think of a hundred."

*Oh my, I'm getting warm and excited just hearing Lucas say things like "if we had the time." Mr. Lucas, take your time. I have all the time you need.*

"I was flying for Peterson and Peterson at the time, and the chief pilot was a little different. I got a call from him early one morning, asking me to take a flight leaving at nine o'clock. His name was Bud, but everyone called him 'Bud the dud'—not to his face, of course. Anyway, I got to the airport at eight thirty and was told that we were ready to go, and that we would leave as soon as the passengers boarded. At about eight fifty, they arrived and we departed. Somewhere around twelve thousand feet, Bud got up, handed me a scrap of paper—the corner of a piece of notepaper he'd torn off—and said, 'These are the navigation frequencies you need. Level off at twenty-five thousand feet; I'll be back.' With that, Bud left the cockpit, went into the cabin, and shut the door. I didn't have a clue where we were going. I had never flown with Bud, I didn't know him, and he didn't know me. There I was—at twenty-five thousand feet, in the cockpit by myself, not knowing the destination—while the chief pilot hobnobbed with execs in the back. That doesn't sound like much, but for someone who likes to be in control, like a pilot, it was an experience you can't forget."

Heather just listened without saying a word. Lucas looked at his watch and said, somewhat startled, "My God, it's already three in the morning and I have school!"

As Lucas set down his glass and rose from the couch, he turned to Heather and said, "Heather, this was great. Let's get together again sometime. I still owe you a story, you know."

"Sure would love to get together; just say when."

Both made it to the door, but neither knew just how to best say good-bye. Lucas put his left hand on Heather's right shoulder, leaned toward her, and gave her a kiss on her forehead. Without another word, he swung around and left. Heather was too taken back by the turn of events to even move. Instead, she leaned back against the closed door and slid down to sit on the floor.

# CHAPTER SIX

## Passion in The Sky

❧

Heather's next evening at work was pretty quiet, with the usual hotshots and playful pilots passing through. Between flirtations with her customers, it seemed like she just made endless pots of coffee and bags of popcorn. She could never figure out why pilots drank gallons of coffee and ate tons of popcorn, as if the two were essential survival foods. She decided to ask Lucas the next time she saw him.

In the blink of an eye, her evening improved. From her desk, she could see Lucas pull into the parking lot. Mesmerized by the sight of him, she didn't blink as Lucas got out of his bright-red Corvette. Heather suddenly realized that he had either arrived earlier than usual, or that it was later than she thought. She checked a nearby clock and found that he was early, which was most unusual for Lucas.

As he approached the door, Heather looked away, not wanting Lucas to know that she'd been watching him, must less awaiting his arrival. Grabbing a few gas bills, she turned slightly away from the door and began filing them. The cabinet was low, allowing her to remain seated.

Lucas walked straight to the counter. Not wanting to make a big deal of his arrival, he approached the counter quietly, and then just stood there watching Heather.

He stood just out of her line of sight. She'd heard the door open, so she knew he had entered the lobby. She kept listening intently to track his movements, but didn't enjoy much success. Her curiosity finally got the best of her: she turned her head just enough to find him standing there.

"I thought I heard someone come in," Heather said as she swung around to face Lucas.

"I didn't want to disturb you; you looked like you were in the middle of something, so I just watched." *Damn,* Lucas thought. *She is one beautiful, sexy young lady. Do I actually see a hint of white panties up there? Jeez, I love those miniskirts! How does nature create such beauty?*

"You wouldn't have disrupted me. I'd have been disappointed had you not stopped by."

"Well, you've been on my mind, and I just wanted to swing by and say hi."

"Glad you did; until now, this has been a forgettable day."

Lucas could hardly take his eyes off of Heather, who was still seated in her signature miniskirt. He was overwhelmed with feelings that are typically associated with seeing a beautiful woman in a mini skirt. His body felt tingly, and sexually aroused by the sight of her—especially her beautiful, soft legs protruding from beneath her skirt. With legs crossed, her skirt barely covered her privates. Physical beauty isn't everything, but it was easy to see why every pilot in the Midwest talked about the receptionists at Gold Coast Aviation. Lucas wondered how he could have ever ignored this beautiful young lady, especially knowing that she had the hots for him. His disappointment in himself intensified when he realized that he almost allowed his stupidity to come between Mike and himself. *All that time, Mike was just trying to do what he thought was in my best interest. And, I was an ass to both Mike and Heather. How can I ever make things right?*

"I know this is short notice," Lucas said, "but we have a run down to Atlanta tonight. The weather is nice and, well, if you wanted to, you could sleep on our way down, back, or both. What do you think? Want to come along?"

There was no need to think twice, no need to hesitate. Heather, with the enthusiasm of a six-year-old getting her first puppy, accepted the invite.

"Fantastic!" said Lucas. "We'll be leaving around ten thirty. I got here a little early, hoping you would say yes. Let me get things squared away with the plane, and then maybe we can spend some time together before I go to work."

"Great! When I get off work, I'll go to the office or look for you around the plane."

Heather couldn't believe that her persistence was paying off. She and Lucas were actually talking and doing things together, even if he was working. Knowing how challenging her road had been so far, she was glad to take whatever she could get, even if that just meant flying with him in the middle of the night.

Lucas headed to the office and picked up several documents before proceeding to the Convair. That hunk of aluminum, engines, and electronics was considered a workhorse by those in the airplane business. Pilots found it reliable and stable. That night, Lucas saw a magical carriage rather than a workhorse. It was a carriage that would carry the woman who had captured his attention—who had excited every male hormone in his body. It would carry them into the heavens above, a world where only the two of them existed.

After a few seconds, his thoughts returned to earth. Just moments ago, embarrassment had been a real possibility due to the bulge in his pants. That had been the result of nothing more than seeing Heather at her desk. Now, Lucas wondered how he could concentrate on flying the plane with her consuming his every thought.

Lucas went through his usual preflight checklist. Following his inspection of the plane's exterior, Lucas shifted his attention to the cabin, making sure the cargo tie-downs were in place so that once the cargo arrived, the loading would go smoothly. Unlike other trips, he dropped a short row of sling seats along the left side of the cabin, which would be out of the way of the cargo once loaded. He located several blankets and a pillow, in case Heather wanted to get some sleep during the trip. Finished with his preflight activities, he retreated to the office, hoping he could spend a little time with Heather before they left.

While Lucas was prepping the plane, Autumn came in to relieve Heather.

"Autumn," Heather said. "You won't believe it; Lucas stopped by a little while ago and asked me to go with them tonight."

"Are you going?" responded Autumn.

"Does a bear poop in the woods? Of course I'm going. I've been trying to get Lucas's attention for months."

"So you're horny?" asked Autumn.

"Let's just say I get tongue tied when he's around; I feel self-conscious just talking to him. If you felt that way about some guy, wouldn't you try to get to know him?"

"So you're not just horny?"

"No, I like the guy. What's this 'horny' stuff?"

"Well, I can't say what I would do in your case, since a guy has never made me feel self-conscious, tongue-tied, or anything but horny."

"Autumn, I'm sure there was some guy, somewhere, who struck a nerve other than the one between your legs."

"Don't bet on it. If guys didn't have dicks, there wouldn't be any need for them."

"Autumn, don't you just enjoy their company sometimes?"

"Nope."

"So you don't know what I'm going through, do you?"

"Not really, but I wish you luck. My track record with these pilots hasn't been good. They all look good until you get to know them—but you hang in there and keep me posted."

"Will do. Right now I'm going to try to find Lucas."

Lucas returned to the office, but instead of finding Heather, he found Mike reviewing material important to the night's flight—weather, routing, the maintenance record of the Convair, and those sorts of things. Lucas stuck his head in the door and asked Mike if he had seen Heather.

"Nope. She wasn't at the front desk when I came through, either. Why you ask?" With a gleam in his eye, he asked, "Things go well the other night? Get a little?"

"Things went well and no, I didn't get any!"

"Well, something's up or you wouldn't be looking for Heather. Come on, what's going on?"

"I just thought she may enjoy going with us tonight, so I invited her."

"You invited her to go tonight? You can't do that. The chief of operations is going with us tonight. How do you plan to explain this gorgeous young girl in the cockpit?" After a short pause he added, "Just joking! But something's definitely going on; you should have seen the look on your face!"

"All right. I think she's cool. I was wrong to resist getting to know her. It pains me to say this, but I owe you one. Feel better now? OK, here's the deal: I do want the airline job. School is a challenge, the homework is a challenge, and flying all night isn't exactly a bowl of cherries. When it comes to dating, well, I haven't had much time for girls since high school."

"Lucas, you're fucked up! You're a college student, for Christ's sake."

"I'm an adult who has returned to school while working. That doesn't exactly make me a *college student*."

"Forget the student thing; you are young! You are supposed to get drunk on Friday nights and get laid three times a week, maybe four. What are you going to do, wait until you get that airline job—and are flying every day of the week—to put your dipstick in the well? Is that your plan? You dickhead! You should be like the rest of your friends, trying to get in every skirt you meet. This is what young people do. That's what college is for. I know you're not a real college student, but that doesn't mean you can't act like one! Didn't anyone tell you that? Remember that night you and I got drunk?"

"Which time?"

"You dickhead, the time we got the tattoos."

"Sure I remember it; how could I ever forget it? I have a tattoo to remind me of it, thanks to you!"

"Well, get your head out of your ass, you hypocrite. What did you insist that tattoo say?"

"All right, I get your point. I already admitted to screwing up."

"What the fuck does it say?"

"'If it has wings, fly it,'" Lucas quoted. "'If it wears a skirt, fuck it.'"

"Lucas, you're young. Live your own words. And incidentally, I didn't force you to get that tattoo."

"All right, but I don't want to fuck Heather."

"What?"

"I don't want to fuck Heather. I want to make love to her."

"Oh shit, your dick gets hard and you're fucking in love? Do you think every time some gal spreads her legs it's because she's in love? Get the fuck out of here!"

"Mike, where do you get off talking to me like that? How old are you?"

"None of your fucking business."

"You're fifty-seven years old, you're an alcoholic, and have been divorced three times. You get a boner and think you have to screw the first woman you see. And you think you have the right to be giving me advice."

"Lucas, you're fucking wet behind the ears. Get your ass out of here."

Not wanting the atmosphere to become more toxic than it had already become, Lucas returned to the Convair without saying another word.

Once the flight was underway, Mike, Lucas, and Heather engaged in normal, civil conversation. No one would ever know that Mike and Lucas had had words earlier. The atmosphere was light and pleasant.

Heather was in heaven knowing that she was on this trip because Lucas had personally invited her. Lucas was also pleased to know that Heather had accepted his invitation. Even Mike was pleased, because he knew that he had played a significant role in bringing the two together, even if it hadn't always been easy.

The trip was long, and Lucas eventually not only needed a bathroom break, but had begun to feel his legs getting numb, his feet going to sleep and as though his bottom was glued to the seat. After making sure Mike had the plane, Lucas asked Heather to descend from her perch on the jump seat so he could maneuver past her to get to the bathroom in the rear of the plane.

Bathroom break over and circulation restored to his legs, Lucas returned to the cockpit. As he approached the cockpit from the rear of the plane, he could see Heather's profile in the dim cockpit. She was standing in the aisle, watching whatever was taking place up front.

He stopped to watch. He couldn't help but think, *What a beautiful lady.* She appeared so mysterious; the outline of her body wasn't well-defined, so only his knowledge of her allowed his mind to fill in the shadows. She'd spread her legs a little to stabilize her. She also held on to the two front seats.

Lucas entered the cockpit area, and Heather could feel him as he approached her from behind. The warmth from his body announced his arrival. Heather began to reposition herself, so he could return to his flying duties. When it became apparent he didn't intend to walk by her, she resumed her original stance. Lucas stood directly behind Heather, staring over her right shoulder.

Rather than holding onto the plane, he held Heather's hips and leaned gently against her. His face toyed with the hair tucked behind her right ear. Her scent was uniquely Heather, subtle like that of a bouquet of freshly cut flowers.

She could feel vibrations not only through direct contact with the plane, but through Lucas as well. She could feel his warm breath on her right ear. It was the most sensual moment she had ever experienced. Her whole body became sensitive to Lucas's every movement, to his breathing, to the way he held her. Lucas was also becoming excited by their closeness. The rhythmic wave passing through their bodies from the plane's vibration created a sensation he'd never before experienced. Lucas began to slowly move his hands downward and forward, stopping only when reaching the unmistakable curves of her groin.

Heather's heart raced. Not knowing what was going to happen next, she simply relaxed and gave way to Lucas's sexual advances.

Lucas continued to explore Heather's body, from her tummy to her groin. He toyed with her pubic area, well-defined through her thin skirt. He quickly discovered that Heather wasn't wearing panties.

Suddenly, Heather leaned her head back while pushing her backside hard against Lucas's swollen cock. She began to move in harmony with Lucas's hands, saying "yes" to his stroking movement, encouraging further exploration. Her eyes closed as she let herself be consumed by Lucas's every movement.

Only the thickness of a silk skirt separated his fingers from the wetness between Heather's legs. As he explored her groin, he could feel Heather spread her legs ever so slightly to encourage his exploration. Accepting her invitation, Lucas slid his hand beneath her skirt and a finger into the folds of her wetness, where he could feel the silky smoothness of her love juices.

Without warning, Mike turned to partly face the couple. He bellowed, "Come on, guys; knock it off. We're almost home. You can get a room and fuck all night once we're there, but right now I need to take a piss."

Mike's intrusion was a cold reminder to both of them that their behavior was not appropriate, at least at that moment.

Lucas quickly took his seat, buckled up, and announced that he had the plane. Lucas couldn't get over what had taken place. He'd been the one to first object to Heather coming along, under the pretense that he didn't need the distraction. Still excited, he had to force himself to focus on the task at hand as the bulge in his pants began to subside. Even his hands were a distraction—he would occasionally stare at them as though they were separate from the rest of his body. After all, they had actually fondled Heather's pubic area, a feat that had previously only taken place in his mind.

Mike chuckled on the inside about Lucas and Heather. Lucas had been so stubborn about getting involved with Heather, and now he couldn't keep his hands off her. Mike wasn't trying to be cruel by tossing water on their little party, but he really did have to take a piss.

Heather, waiting for Mike to return, stood there silent and embarrassed.

For the rest of the trip, only Mike and Lucas spoke, and then only as they went about their duties. Their gentlemen's code allowed both of them to write off the incident.

# CHAPTER SEVEN
## *The Payoff*

❧

Heather couldn't stop thinking about her encounter with Lucas on the plane.

*Those few minutes were so intense*, she often thought, *that no one else would understand. I'll never forget that encounter. I can't help but wonder if we will ever be able to recapture that special moment and make everything around us disappear, leaving only the two of us in our own little world. Even if we attempted to duplicate that special moment, it would probably fall short of my expectations. Special moments often just happen, and can seldom be planned, much less duplicated.*

The sight of Lucas entering the lobby jolted Heather from her daze. Although aware of her new tendency to drift off and daydream about him, Heather was confident that no one had noticed.

"Hey, Heather!" Lucas called. "T.G.I.F.! Want to come over to my place tomorrow night and let me show you what a good cook I am?"

"Sure, love to. What time?"

"Is six too early?"

"Not at all. What should I bring?"

"Your toothbrush! Just joking. Don't bring anything but your beautiful smile."

"All right, see you tomorrow. Oh wait—I need your address, and directions might be helpful," with concern in the tone of Heathers voice.

"Sure," Lucas said, "that would probably help. I'll write them down. Have you seen Mike yet?"

"He passed through several minutes ago."

"Thanks. See you tomorrow night."

Lucas headed straight to the office, walking with purpose. His face was stern. Reaching the office door, he opened it with a force that could have pulled it from its hinges.

Mike looked up from the papers spread across his desk, somewhat startled by the manner in which the door had been opened. Lucas walked straight up to Mike and tossed an envelope onto his desk. The letter nearly slid off into Mike's lap. Only Mike's quick reflexes prevented the envelope from leaving the desk. Mike picked up the envelope and, in an agitated tone, said "What the fuck is this?"

"You see who it's from?" responded Lucas.

"Yeah. It's from the feds."

"Well, open it and read it."

Mike pulled the letter out of the opened envelope. He unfolded the paper and began to read. The letter was addressed to Lucas and read, in part, "Based on a recent ramp check, we discovered you flew Convair N3713P and that it had not had the hundred-hour inspection. This is a violation of FAR 91.409(b). Please respond to this notice within ten days to avoid administrative action."

"Mike," Lucas said coldly. "Think before you speak; I'm pissed."

"When did you get this?"

"Today. Didn't you get one just like it?"

"No. I haven't seen anything like this. Guess it's coming; we've both been flying the Convair."

"Look, Mike, I can't have this. Global is conducting another background check, and if this creates a problem with Global, someone will pay. Besides, I'm not even the one responsible for checking the maintenance records."

"Lucas, relax. As I see it, we both have the same problem."

Lucas said, "We don't have the same problem! Don't you check those maintenance records every time before we fly?"

"I do, and I don't understand. Lucas, why don't you go ahead and take care of the preflight and I'll finish up here. When we get back, I'll dig into these records and see what I can find. Sound like a plan?"

Still agitated, Lucas just said, "I don't know that we can do anything else at this time of night. See ya at the plane."

Lucas may have been agitated, but Heather could only wait for the night to crawl by while she anticipated her date with Lucas the next night. Finally, Heather saw Autumn parking, which was the first real sign that the evening had come to an end. It meant she could allow her thoughts to focus on Saturday night without feeling guilty.

"Hey, Autumn," she said brightly. "How you doing tonight?"

"I'm fine, but I want to hear about your trip to Atlanta. Join the mile-high club?"

"No," Heather answered in a matter-of-fact voice.

"Steve in the shop told me he found the sling seat lowered, with a pillow and blankets on it. I assumed you two did the deed."

"No. I've decided that a plane isn't the place to get laid, at least not by someone who's supposed to be flying it."

"Didn't you have any fun?" Autumn asked with a puzzled tone.

"Autumn, I don't kiss and tell."

"That means you have something to share."

"Not really. I just meant that if I *did* have something to say, if something *did* happen, I wouldn't talk about it. That stuff is personal."

"Come clean, Heather. I want to hear about that personal stuff."

"There isn't any personal stuff." *She is relentless. I know she isn't going to drop this. If I don't give her something tonight she'll never leave me alone. Worse yet, she may corner Lucas.*

"Yes, there is. You have that look. You can't bullshit a bullshitter. I know when you are holding something back."

"OK, but you have to keep this to yourself. Promise?"

"Promise. Not a word to anyone."

"Autumn, it was unbelievable. It was like being felt up in the middle of a movie theater."

"I've never been felt up in a movie theater, but the thought is exciting," muttered Autumn.

"I don't know how to explain it. I guess it felt like I was getting away with something—being naughty or wicked or something. We were right there in the cockpit and Lucas started playing with me. I almost came in my pants, but I didn't have any on.

"Was Mike there?"

"Of course he was. Where else would he have been?"

"I don't know. You said you had your stuff exposed to the world. What was he doing? Watching?"

"No, it wasn't like that. My business wasn't exposed to the world."

"You said you didn't have any pants on, so tell me: What were you doing?"

"Lucas and I were standing in the aisle right behind the pilots' seats. Lucas reached around and started rubbing me. My privates got wet and, like I said, I almost climaxed. It was one of those moments that will probably never happen again. I have a date with him tomorrow night. Think I'll get laid?"

"Forget tomorrow night. I still want to hear more about what took place in the plane. I understand *you* standing behind the pilot seats, but what was Lucas doing there? Wasn't he supposed to be *in* one of those seats?"

"He had to take a leak and had just come back."

"So Mike wasn't watching? What was he doing?"

"He was flying the plane."

"Oh, OK. Mike was flying the plane while you two were getting your rocks off right behind him."

"That makes it sound really weird. In reality, everything felt very natural, the way it developed and all."

"OK. You say you have a date with Lucas. I thought he wasn't dating?"

"Getting a date wasn't easy. I've been trying to get his attention for months, much less a date."

"Well, I hope you get laid. I understand he's good in the sack. So where you going?"

"His place. Now it's your turn to talk, Autumn," said Heather with a stern tone in her voice. "Do you know someone who had a relationship with him?"

"No, it's just what I've heard."

"Who from? Give the specifics. You're holding out on me."

"I don't know; I just heard it from someone. I don't much pay attention that kind of stuff. Heather, I predict you'll get laid."

"It's been a long time. Hope I remember how to do it."

"Heather, people don't forget that stuff. How long has it been?"

"Probably three years. I had just started college and was mostly confused—like most kids, I think. I had never had sex, and I guess I just thought I was expected to do it. We only did it three times, and I didn't find it particularly fun. He wasn't really that wonderful."

"That was the problem—the wrong guy. But are you telling me that you've only fucked some guy three times and you're in your early twenties? Do you rub one out every once in a while—you know, masturbate?"

"No. I told you I don't have much experience with sex."

"I know, but masturbating doesn't have anything to do with having sex. It has everything to do with giving yourself pleasure without having sex. I probably get it on by myself at least once a week. Anyway, I'm surprised you've only had sex three times in your life. I try to get laid at least three times a week."

"Three times a week! Are you kidding me? You don't even have a steady boyfriend. Do you even know the guys you're doing?"

"Generally. Mostly we're on-and-off lovers just trying to keep things simple. You know, no strings attached."

"Whatever makes you happy. As for me, what can I say? My first experience put me on guard. I decided to be pickier about the next guy I spread my legs for. In all honesty, I've got this thing for Lucas, but don't even know him. I'm not sure why he has the effect on me that he does. What do you think, Autumn? I'm just horny?"

"No, you're not just horny. Sounds like there may be some chemistry there. Although horny is a possibility."

Saturday night finally arrived.

Heather didn't consider herself a particularly good navigator. As a result, she usually left her apartment thirty minutes earlier than any other person would. She also kept instructions and a map neatly placed on the passenger seat, for when a quick review became necessary—a quick review being the norm, not the exception.

A little before six o'clock on Saturday night, Heather reached the most challenging part of her journey—finding Lucas's apartment among what looked like a thousand identical apartments with identical doors, identical patios, identical everything. His complex exemplified the term "cookie-cutter housing." *If a person comes home here after having a little too much to drink, who knows where they'd end up?* She thinks to herself.

Lucas told her not to bring anything, and she almost complied. Perhaps it was wishful thinking, but Heather decided to pack a small bag to prepare for the remote possibility that she might spend the night. The thought of spending the night made the hair on her arms stand erect. Just packing the overnight bag sparked a sexual arousal that she couldn't have anticipated. None of this came as a surprise to Heather, since she had been in a state of arousal all afternoon—anything seemed possible. At the moment, Heather had one thing on her mind: having a satisfying evening with the person who made her heart skip a beat just by looking into his deep, mysterious, penetrating, brown eyes.

Preparations for the evening began when she started to put her already near-perfect body into a state she thought of as "date night ready." "Date night ready" included plucking her eyebrows and ensuring every hair on her head was in place. During this part of the ritual, she became thankful that her hair was short and easy to manage. After finishing her head, she moved south. Clear polish for her nails—all twenty; shaved legs; and a touch-up of her bikini area, just in case. The final step before slipping into her freshly cleaned miniskirt was to cover her body in her favorite lotion, to ensure the sensuality of her skin and to add a hint of fragrance.

Before closing her overnight bag and waltzing out the door, Heather quickly checked to be sure she had everything—a fresh pair of panties, deodorant, toothbrush, toothpaste so she wouldn't feel intrusive, and a pair of running pants, pull-over sleeveless shirt, socks, and shoes.

Not knowing which apartment was Lucas's, and unable to see the addresses, she decided to simply look for his red Corvette. After cruising the parking lots for about fifteen minutes, she spotted his glistening Corvette about a block away, on her side of the street. Directly in front of his car was Lucas, standing on his patio as though on the lookout for someone who could be lost.

As soon as she parked in the visitor spot next to Lucas's car, he appeared to open her door. Her overnight bag, cleverly disguised as a large purse, sat next to her. She grabbed her purse with her right hand, allowing Lucas to assist her by taking her left hand as she swung out of the car.

"I see you found the place. Have much trouble?" Lucas asked as he gave Heather a hug and a kiss on her head.

"Not really; just didn't know exactly where I was going until I got here."

"Well, come on in and let me show you around."

They entered the apartment through a sliding door that led directly into a family room, complete with a large-screen television and fireplace. Straight past the family room was a small living room. A cozy kitchen was on the left, with access to both the family room and the living room. These three rooms formed a horseshoe, with the kitchen at the closed end. From the family room, and opposite the kitchen, was a passage that led to another hallway perpendicular to it. Turning left led to the master bedroom. To the right was a bathroom, and at the end was a guest room. The walls were abundantly decorated with many pictures taken by Lucas. The pictures ranged from aviation-related to photographs of scenery from the many locations his job had taken him. Decor within the apartment was much more sophisticated than would be expected from a single guy in his twenties who lived by himself.

"Why don't you have a seat while I finish dinner?" he asked Heather. "Something to drink?"

"Got wine?"

"I have riesling, merlot, and a blackberry wine. Any of those sound OK? I have Select and Amber Bock beer, or I could make a pitcher of margaritas."

"OK, you talked me into it—I'll take a pitcher of margaritas."

"Aren't you the funny one? Would you like salt on your pitcher?"

"Actually no, but thanks for asking. Lucas, can I help with something? I feel guilty just sitting here with you doing all the work." *Now I know I've been dating the wrong guys; Lucas is actually waiting on me. And cooking? Is it possible I'm dreaming? Wonder why he doesn't have a girlfriend!*

"Not at all! You relax; I'll take care of everything. The remote's on the table, in case you want to catch the news."

While Lucas retreated to the kitchen to put the finishing touches on dinner and to prepare the margaritas, Heather took a seat on the leather couch perpendicular to the fireplace and directly in front of the television.

"Ever use your fireplace in the summer?" Heather asked.

"All the time—I love to relax in front of it and just watch the flames do their dance. I find it very relaxing. I thought about asking you to bring a swimsuit with you, but it looks like we're going to get some weather in here in the next couple of hours, so we may be using the fireplace instead of taking a dip."

"That would have been fun. I love to swim, or at least get some sun. Sitting in front of a fireplace sounds nice too. Use the pool much?" *He said he enjoys watching the flames dance; could Lucas actually have a sensitive side? Swimming pool...bet I could get attention in there!*

"All the time; perhaps we can take a dip the next time you come over."

"That would be fun! Just say when, and I'll be here." Heather has to pinch herself. *Did he actually say the next time I come over? Things seem to working out better than I imagined.*

From her vantage point on the couch, Heather surveyed the apartment. This was the first time Heather had been in a real apartment belonging to a man. While in school, she had sometimes gone to a guy's apartment, but it was a mess with little furniture. TV trays were used for lamp tables, with metal folding chairs scattered about. The bed was just a mattress lying on the floor. Recounting that affair, Heather now knew why they only screwed three times. Turned out his apartment was as uninviting as he was.

Recognizing that Lucas was only a few years older than she, Heather became very aware that he seemed to be much more financially secure than she, and she began to feel envious.

Lucas returned with a margarita in one hand and a glass of merlot in the other.

"Heather, would you take a couple of those coasters and set them out on the table? I'm going to let the sauce simmer another twenty minutes, then we'll be ready to eat. Hungry? Like spaghetti?" Lucas put the drinks on the coasters and joined Heather on the couch.

"Yes and yes. I love spaghetti."

"Well, relax; it'll be ready shortly."

"So, Lucas, I'd like you to finish telling me about your exciting flights—the stories you started at my place—but I also want to know more about Mike. He seems a little crusty on the outside, but seems to have a good heart."

"Mike is a trip. He is one interesting person. I'm not sure where to start. You're right on target when you say he's a little crusty. Mike drives people away. I'm not sure he has any real friends. I'm probably as close a friend as he has. We go drinking every once in a while, when we have a night off. It's not uncommon for both of us to get stumbling drunk. I'm surprised we haven't killed ourselves in the process. But Mike doesn't need to go out drinking to get drunk. In fact, I think he stays drunk."

"Has he ever tried to get help?"

"I don't think so. He was in the service, and I get the impression that's when he started drinking and just became a boozer ever since. He flew a gunship in Iraq, toward the end of that conflict. I don't know if it was the war that drove him to the bottle or something else."

"How old is he?"

"Fifty-seven, but he looks and acts like he's older."

"Don't you guys have to get a physical to fly?"

"Every six months."

With a puzzled look, she asked, "Why hasn't his drinking problem come out in a physical?"

"Can't answer that one; have no idea." Lucas paused and then said, "You're also right when you say that he has a heart. Under that crusty exterior is a nice guy. He really cares about his flying partner, despite his grumpy appearance. When not under the influence, he's one hell of a pilot."

"And when he's drunk?"

"He falls asleep and I end up flying the plane myself. As for his personal life, he's been married three times, but never had kids of his own. His second wife had a son, but I don't think he ever sees him or even stays in touch. He lives by himself in an apartment in Kirkwood. It's a nice place, but is definitely lacking any kind of a theme, mostly just random furniture—nothing fancy. I don't know for sure, but I don't think he has had a girlfriend since I've known him."

"Do you think that's why he is so grumpy? That is, do you think he needs a girlfriend?"

"Not sure. If he had someone, she probably wouldn't stick around more than a week or two."

"That's too bad," responded Heather, sadly. "Now tell me about your flying experiences—something exciting."

"Heather, exciting is in the eye of the beholder."

"OK, something not routine. You know what I mean."

"If you recall, I've had many memorable flights; some just seem to stay with me longer than others. I guess I'll never forget one trip to Mansfield, Ohio. We were landing in a blizzard. During our approach, my partner flew the plane and I watched for the runway. The only thing I could see were snowflakes flying past the windshield. It was like seeing a million horizontal white streaks against a solid white backdrop. Without the instruments, we wouldn't have had any idea if we were at a thousand feet or ten thousand feet.

"Anyway, the altimeter was putting us within about three hundred feet of the runway when I saw the sequence flashers. Those are the bright lights that flash much like the flash on cameras; they lead you straight to the runway. The lights are so bright, they'll shine through the thickest fog. I can still remember the image of the runway. It was almost like someone had taken a brush and painted an obscure picture of a runway threshold. Beyond the touchdown area, blowing snow prevented the runway from being completely clear. At any given point on the runway, I could only see about forty percent of the surface. To make the landing even more difficult, the visibility was very poor, which prevented the runway boundary from being well defined. It was like it had been swallowed by the surrounding white. From my first sighting to touchdown was only a matter of seconds. The runway's centerline was partly covered with blowing snow, but we made it. The interesting part of the trip was when we returned to Spirit that same day. It had continued snowing and remained cold all day. The takeoff was normal except for the blowing snow and poor visibility."

Heather occasionally closed her eyes in an attempt to visualize what Lucas was describing, but without ever witnessing what she was hearing, it was hard for her imagination to take over and fill in the gaps.

"We climbed through the snowstorm," Lucas continued, "and once on top we had a beautiful day, with bright sun and a dark blue sky. The transformation was incredible—one second we were in heavy snow, the next we were reaching for our sunglasses. I remember it was bitter cold. I'm guessing maybe fifty below zero at twenty-six thousand. St. Louis was in the teens. Everything during the landing was normal until we touched down. We blew all four tires on the main gear at touchdown. I guess that we'd packed the wheels and brakes with snow during takeoff. Since we were in freezing weather, nothing melted or blew away. That King Air almost took us for a ride in the cornfield, but we got it stopped before we ran off the runway. We had to leave the plane on the runway, and a car was sent out to pick us up."

"Wow! Were you scared?"

"Nope. Didn't have time to think about possible consequences, just react to what was happening. Now let's go get a bite to eat. Incidentally, you are looking radiant tonight. I love your outfit."

"Thanks! You know fashion is my passion."

"You convinced me."

"Will you tell me more about your flying experiences? How and when did you get started?"

"Sure. Don't know that it's the sort of thing people talk about over dinner, but I would be happy to tell you more. You know, one of the things I like about flying is the range of experiences, the sights that are unique at any given moment. That's probably true for most pilots, and that's also why most pilots never hesitate to tell their stories. I sometimes try to share my experiences, but I'm not sure I'm very successful. I'm not always sure I have the words to share what I see and feel up there.

Sometimes I wonder if anyone is even listening. If they are, they're probably wishing this joker would shut up."

"Well, don't shut up! I would love to hear everything you have to say. I want to know all about you."

"Well, for as long as I can remember I've loved airplanes. When I was a kid, I would spend my money on model airplanes, build them, and have them sitting all around my bedroom. When I turned sixteen, I got a job at St. Charles Airport pumping gas into small planes. While working there I took flying lessons. When I turned seventeen, I got my private pilot license. From there I got my commercial certificate, multi-engine, and instrument ratings. Then I picked up my ground instructor, flight instructor and instrument instructor ratings. For a while, I spent a lot of time teaching flying and doing charter work. You really learn how to fly when you teach someone else how to do it. Anyway, enough about me. What about you?"

"No, me later. Tell me more."

"What else do you want to know?"

"What was your first flight like?"

After a short period of reflection, Lucas said, "'Liberating' is the best word I can think of to describe the flight. I can remember it like it was yesterday. That seat next to me was really empty. I was by myself. While thrilled to be the only one in the plane, I had no idea how lonely I could feel. It was liberating because it gave me a level of confidence that I probably wouldn't have today had that flight not happened. My success or failure that day was up to me and me alone. I have since discovered that is true of most things in life."

"How old were you? "

"Sixteen."

"Wow. While most people are learning how to drive, you were learning how to fly. Were you ever scared?"

"Once. I thought I was going to die. Ready for dessert?"

"My compliments to the chef! The spaghetti was fantastic—perfect."

"Glad you enjoyed it."

"Dessert sounds great, but I want to hear about the time you were scared. Can I help get something?"

"Nope, I already have it put together. Be right back with goodies and a story."

"I'll be waiting," responds Heather.

"Hope you like crème brûlée—made it a little while ago!" Lucas yells from the kitchen.

"I love it. Did you know that, or is this just my lucky night?"

"Heather, for now let's just say this is your lucky night," said Lucas as he placed the dessert on the empty place mat. If not yours, I'm thinking this is going to be *my* lucky night, Lucas thinks to himself. Lucas returned to his chair and they both indulged in Lucas's creation.

"Here we go," Lucas said. "This will be the last story for the night. I was taking four other pilots down to Vero Beach in Florida. We were moving right along on a pretty, moonlit night, but could see lightning in the distance. Funny thing about lightning at night is without radar you never know how far away it is—it could be ten miles or a hundred. Anyway, we were talking to Center, the radar folks, and they didn't have anything for us. We were enjoying a nice, smooth flight when we started picking up light rain on the windshield. Within seconds, we were in the cell of a thunderstorm. I think I could actually hear the wind as the air currents changed around the plane. It may be my imagination, but I have this image of the rain streaming *down* the side window instead of running horizontally as it should. The plane was almost uncontrollable. My instincts said to turn, and about as fast as we entered the storm, we flew out the side. The rain stopped instantly, and we once again had a moonlit night and smooth air. And most importantly, five pilots lived to fly again. Now that's the end of all my stories."

"I'm envious."

"Because you haven't flown into a thunderstorm?"

"No I'm envious because at the age of twenty-nine you have had experiences few people ever will. I wonder if I will ever do anything that someone else would find interesting."

Lucas turned his head slightly to the right. "Speaking of thunderstorms," he said, "hear the thunder? Sounds like a big one. Did you put your windows up in the car?"

"Sure did. I always close and lock my car when I leave it."

"That rascal's close." As the rumbling thunder caused the frames on the wall to rattle, Lucas got up to make sure none were about to fall. None left their anchor on the wall, so Lucas returned to the couch.

Ominous clouds, lightning, and thunder that shook the ground had moved into the Chesterfield area. Storm warning sirens began to sound. At this point, Heather began to wonder whether nature was going to interfere with her pans for a romantic evening, and was reminded of her first flight when weather put a damper on what started out as a romantic flight. At about that time, the lights in the apartment went out.

Watching through the sliding patio door, Lucas and Heather could see that the entire complex had lost power. The frequent lightning sent a chill through Heather. If it weren't for those flashes of lightning, they wouldn't have been able to see anything. As it was, about all they could see was the heavy downpour. To comfort Heather, Lucas placed his right arm around her waist. Lucas's closeness, and his warmth and manly scent did what Lucas intended: it helped Heather relax and took her mind off the storm.

"Heather," he said. "It looks like this storm is going to be around for a while. I'll light the fire and get you another drink; let's enjoy the light show."

"Sounds like a wonderful idea. I'm going to use the restroom first. Is it around the corner to the right?" she asked.

"Yes it is, but let me light a candle for you." As Lucas retreated from the now-lit bathroom, he allowed his mind to wander. *Heather is looking like a million bucks. I wonder what it is in me that she sees. There are dozens, no, make that hundreds of men that Heather could have, yet for some reason I am her chosen, at least for now. I will probably never understand, but I can enjoy the ride until our journey ends. Guess that's something we have in common; neither of us really knows the other person or where this is headed.*

Heather made her way to the candlelit bathroom. Door closed and temporarily in her own world, Heather considered looking in Lucas's medicine cabinet. She wouldn't look for anything in particular, but it seemed like a part of Lucas she had yet to discover. At the moment, Heather was hungry for more information about Lucas, but finally decided that she was content to make small discoveries over time. Bathroom duties completed, she made her way back to the couch and arrived just seconds before Lucas returned.

"I'm going to take my shoes off, Heather," he said. "Why don't you do the same? Let's get comfortable."

Heather's mind was a fireworks display on the fourth of July. She heard "get comfortable" and suddenly had visions of the two naked and cuddled up on the couch. *Back to reality,* she said to herself.

"Good idea!" She tossed her shoes to the side of the couch.

Bright lightning and thunder so loud it rattled the entire building continued relentlessly. The sky throbbed with nature's gigantic light show. The lightning was all but continuous. Heavy rain was being blown against the patio window with enough force to shake the door.

"Heather, it seems like this thunderstorm is stuck right above us. I know this makes you uncomfortable; come over next to me."

"Don't have to ask me twice."

Heather scooted over right next to Lucas. She rested her head on his chest and folded her right arm between them. Her left hand rested on Lucas's belt buckle. Her legs were bent at the knees, allowing her to put her feet on the couch. Lucas's legs were crossed and extending slightly to the left, with his body partially leaning against the right arm of the couch. His left arm was draped behind Heather's left shoulder, and his hand was on Heather's left hip.

"You mentioned earlier that you wanted to do something others would find interesting," he said to her. "My advice is not to worry about other people, but to instead find something that turns your crank, something you have a passion for. Pursue that, and you'll more than likely be happy while others are trying to satisfy other people and disliking what they are doing."

"I already told you I have a passion for fashion, but no one is going to find that interesting."

"Your passion shows every day, and people notice your breathtaking beauty. Your passion speaks to who you are."

"That's nice of you to say, Lucas, but that isn't what I'm talking about. I don't know what I want to do."

As the storm continued, Heather and Lucas sipped their drinks, relaxed, and marveled at the storm's fury. The room was dark except for the ghost-like shadows that appeared with each bolt of lightning, only to disappear as quickly as they formed.

Lucas was uncharacteristically excited by Heather's presence. Her scent was one of purity—very subtle and sweet. Her head was so close to his that it allowed him to tease her with a gentle kiss on the head. He had never touched her hair before, since it was always perfectly in place, but couldn't resist the temptation that night. Not knowing how Heather would react, he gently ran his fingers through her hair, caressing her silky strands. She pulled herself closer to Lucas, signifying acceptance and pleasure.

Heather couldn't believe she was in Lucas's apartment and engaged in such a romantic setting. She fidgeted with his belt buckle with her left hand, as though nervous and not sure what to do with her hands. His buckle, as usual, was large and ornate, making it an easy target in the dark room. Her three margaritas had a negative impact on her willingness to exercise restraint. She wondered if—or when—she should take the lead if Lucas didn't.

Lucas continued to embrace Heather's hip and sometimes caress her stomach. Her dress was silk, making it feel as though he were caressing her bare skin. He could feel the outline of her bikini panties. He'd become aroused. The little general was swelling and had become quite uncomfortable under the constraints of his tight underwear and shorts.

Heather could see the results of her closeness to Lucas. Due to her own arousal, not to mention the margaritas, she gently put her left hand over his straining cock. Unfamiliar with the arrangement of his package, she attempted to manipulate that exciting bulge so that it had the freedom to stretch and grow unobstructed. It became apparent that his clothing wouldn't permit such an adjustment. Without taking her mind off her own pleasure, Heather gently but deliberately unbuckled Lucas's belt, exposing the top of his zipper. Moving slowly, she lifted the zipper and began moving it southward.

Lucas tightened his grip on her hip and held his breath—not consciously, but out of anxiety, because he felt himself losing control. For the first time, Heather was in control of Lucas.

Zipper undone, Heather's left hand returned to Lucas's waist and slid into his underwear. Beginning her southward journey, she encountered the head of Lucas's dick, swollen and rock solid—a mere inch from protruding from his shorts. She was overwhelmed by the size and hardness of his organ of passion. She gently stroked his dick, up and down from his head to his balls, toying with his hair as she paused between the two.

Lucas's state of arousal neared a point of no return. His dick was so hard and swollen, it began to hurt. While Heather fondled Lucas's dick, he stroked Heather's stomach with his left hand, steadily moving to her groin. His touch was gentle. Her skirt was short and presented no obstacle in reaching her panties. He lifted her panties and slid his hand down to where her legs came together, where her groin was moist and hot. He moved his fingers, embracing her every fold and being careful to include her most sensitive area.

Heather was wet  as her excitement built. Both Lucas and Heather were tentative in their explorations, not wanting to appear presumptuous.

"Heather, let's go into the other room. We'll both be more comfortable."

"I'm with you."

Lucas took Heather's hand and led her into the bedroom, where they both began shedding their clothes as they passed through the door. Soon, neither had anything on but goose bumps from the chill in the air.

As they approached the bed, Lucas turned to his right and motioned to Heather that she climb in first. She lay there on her back with her legs slightly spread, her left leg bent at the knee and her left foot against her right knee. Her right leg hung partially off the edge of the bed. The light was dim, casting an inviting, mysterious shadow across her body. She was beautiful. Her skin was soft and smooth, her nipples erect. Concealed only by a shadow was her warm, moist threshold. Her legs seemed to guide Lucas to her place of erotic pleasures. Heather lay there, ready to receive Lucas and immerse herself in whatever pleasurable activities he had in mind.

Lucas leaned onto the bed, though most of his weight remained on his legs, which were planted on the floor. His arms reached out, caressing the inside of Heather's legs as he inched his way toward the treasure that belonged to him on this stormy night—a gift from Heather. Moving slowly and deliberately, Lucas kissed the inside of Heather's legs until he reached her valley of paradise. With the palms of both hands on the insides of her legs, he gently ran his fingers up and down her soft, silky, and moist lips, the doorway to her inner cavern, which held the ultimate gift of pleasure. Heather's excitement was electric; every nerve reached the surface of her skin, making the slightest touch send her into ecstasy.

Lucas used his tongue and fingers like a musician stroking a finely tuned violin. He penetrated her repeatedly with his tongue, while caressing every part of her beautiful lady parts with his fingers. Heather squirmed in an attempt to exercise some control over her pleasure. Both of Heather's hands gripped Lucas's head as she traced his movements. She pulled her legs up by bending them at the knees, keeping her feet on the bed. She dropped her knees outward, spreading her legs wide apart. She arched her back, tightened her body, and, in an exhausted voice, announced her climax.

"Lucas! Lucas," she said. "Stop, you're killing me! Oh, please!" She held his head in an attempt to prevent him from sending her over the edge. "Come up here; let me hold you."

Yielding to her plea, Lucas inched his way on top of her, pausing long enough to repeatedly kiss her tummy. His hands tenderly massaged her hard, erect nipples.

Heather continued to feel her climax rippling through her body. She squeezed Lucas, pulling him even closer. Lucas's arms framed her body, with his hands just under her shoulders. He pulled her close, and they both enjoyed the moment, just holding each other.

The head of his dick gently touched the entrance to her warm and juicy cavern. As they met, Heather was even more eager to take him in. He teased Heather with his cock, gently brushing her. Heather's state of arousal, never having diminished completely, returned with vengeance. Her legs spread wide apart, ready to swallow him with her wet and ravishing passage of love. She pulled him higher, and his cock began to penetrate with ease. Her slit was wet with love juices. With her hands on his buttocks, Heather pulled Lucas in even deeper, arching her back slightly to allow his giant cock to go even deeper into her. Lucas began thrusting his cock in and out, in and out.

Heather moved her pelvis rhythmically, in tune with Lucas. They moaned together, finding immense pleasure in each other.

Heather strained to whisper in Lucas's ear, "It's happening again. I'm coming!" Her body stiffened, she pulled Lucas tightly to her, lifted her pelvis, and held that position so Lucas would have unobstructed access to her. He continued thrusting in and out until he reached an explosive moment of pleasure just seconds after Heather. Waves of electrifying pleasure rippled through their bodies.

Overwhelmed with pleasure, they relaxed ever so slightly, his cock still throbbing deep inside Heather. Her pelvic muscles gripped his dick as the aftershock of her climax returned, time after time. While their juices mingled inside of her, their sweat combined on the outside to form a magical scent.

The only thing remaining after such an emotional and physical encounter was sleep, and sleep they did, with Lucas still inside Heather. In the background, rain fell tranquilly against the window.

In the morning, the thunderstorm that had been so disruptive was nothing but a memory. The sun peeked through the window, gently waking Lucas and Heather. Lucas cuddled Heather from behind, his left arm under her pillow. His right arm was draped over her waist. Heather's hands were overlapping and resting between her breasts.

As their state of consciousness returned to normal, and their heads begin to clear, they both lay there quietly wondering what the other was thinking. Both wondered what had taken place, beyond outrageous sex and orgasms beyond description. Had either offended the other? Had either been too aggressive?

Lucas decided that this wasn't the time to worry. He loved whatever had happened, and as he recalled, Heather did too. Lucas's dick was hard. It had been hard when he went to sleep, and it was hard as he woke up. It began to throb as he pulled Heather closer. Heather made the task easier by reaching over her right thigh to hold Lucas. Neither said anything. Lucas's right hand moved from her soft, warm tummy to between her legs, still moist and so inviting. Lucas began stroking her every curve, inserting his finger to bring Heather to a state of arousal. She began to move in response to Lucas's tender use of his fingers. His dick was sandwiched between her legs, next to her opening. Heather maneuvered her hips so she could feel the head of Lucas's dick toying with the entrance to her pleasure-seeking cavern. Teasing Lucas, she began to move her hips in an orbiting motion, which put the head of his dick just inside of her, and then outside again. Lucas started to breathe heavily. When Heather woke up, she'd still been moist from her own love juices plus Lucas's deposit the previous night. Her wetness had since become the result of passion.

Lucas placed his right hand below her bikini line, directly on her pubic area. As he pulled her toward him, Lucas pushed his hips forward, penetrating deeply into Heather. Doing her part, Heather gave Lucas an unobstructed path by lifting her knees toward her chin. Still spooning, they moved together as a unit. Lucas moved in and out, thrusting his dick deeper and deeper. His left hand toyed with her nipples, which had become sensitive with climax so near. She breathed heavier. Her hips moved in unison with Lucas, and she began to groan and then stiffen as her orgasm overcame her ability to function. The only thing Heather was capable of doing was immersing herself in extreme pleasure. Lucas, feeling Heather's explosion, released into her once again. Once again firing rounds of passion with each throb of his dick, he quivered, with an occasional pause at each shot of euphoria.

Lying there speechless, both exhausted, they simply enjoyed their gifts to one another while holding each other closely. They both let their eyes close and, Lucas still inside of Heather, they momentarily became one.

# CHAPTER EIGHT

## Once is Never Enough

༄

The following Friday was a normal day at the airport for Heather until Lucas arrived.

As Lucas passed through the lobby, he made his way to the counter. "Hey, Heather! Got anything going on this weekend?"

"Not yet. What do you have in mind?"

"The Indy 500 is on Sunday. If you're interested, we could run over there tomorrow, watch the race on Sunday, and come home. Ever been there?"

"No, I haven't, but would love to go."

"Great!" Lucas said. "I won't be back from my trip tonight until around three in the morning. Why don't I run home then, take a nap, and pick you up around eleven? That'll get us there around four. We can check in and still have a little time to explore the area."

"We can do that, but if you want, you could crash at my place when you get back—that might get you to bed a little earlier."

"I can do that, but please don't use the word 'crash.' Let's just call it a sleepover."

With a smile, Heather said, "OK. I'll see you early in the morning. Will you want anything when you get there? Something to eat or drink?"

"Just you. Can you handle that?"

"The question is can *you* handle it," retorted Heather.

"Don't know, but it will be fun finding out. We need to stop talking this way! I won't be able to concentrate on my flying." *Damn, she is looking good tonight! This flying every night is for the birds.*

"Lucas, come here."

Heather reached over the counter and took Lucas's left arm in her hand. She then led him to the end of the counter where the pass-through is located. As they made their way to the end of the counter, Heather surveyed the empty lobby. Then she turned to Lucas and said, "This will give you something to think about while you're up there."

Heather took Lucas's left hand, slid it under her skirt, held it on her pubic area, moved it down, and then began rubbing the soft, warm area between her legs with his fingers. After just a few seconds, she removed his hand and said, "Now go fly your airplane. I'll have more of that waiting for you when you return."

"Sorry to be leaving." Lucas turned around and slowly made his way to the flight office, with a large coffee in one hand and a swollen dick in his pants.

Lucas took his time getting to the office, allowing time for the little general to relax. Mike was already in the office going through some of the preflight paperwork.

"So, Mike, what did you discover about the maintenance record? Incidentally, I heard from Global and I will have another interview scheduled for me in the near future, so I'll need some time off."

"Yeah, OK. Remind me of that a few days before you need off. I went back through everything and found a worksheet indicating that the hundred-hour inspection had been done, but apparently it had never been entered into the aircraft logbook."

"That should clear us, shouldn't it?"

"As far as I can determine, it looks like it's a record-keeping problem in maintenance."

"How do we get the feds to recognize that?"

"Not sure; I'll work on that tomorrow."

"Don't forget I have my interview coming up, so this must be cleared up by then. I can't let anything like this get between me and that job."

"All I can promise is that I'll do my best. Don't overlook *your* role in this process. You know your name is on this citation, too."

"I just want this fixed."

Despite Lucas's discussion with Mike, his concern about Global, and his preoccupation with Heather, the flight that evening went smoothly.

Upon arriving back in St. Louis, Lucas finished his pilot duties and then headed off to Heather's apartment.

When he arrived at Heather's place, there wasn't a single apartment with a light on. After parking his car next to Heather's, Lucas was careful not to make any noise and disturb the neighbors. He was startled when the door opened. On the other side of the door stood Heather, wearing only a seductive smile and a large bow covering her pubic area.

Lucas stepped in, wrapped his arms around her waist, and kicked the door closed. They gave one another a long, lingering kiss, as though they had not seen each other in years.

Lucas still held Heather, and their lips were still fused together, when Heather, with both hands, unzipped his pants and felt his cock grow to an enormous size. While they embraced, Heather wondered how Lucas's cock managed to penetrate her so easily before.

Heather continued fondling Lucas's dick until he withdrew his lips to catch his breath. Heather's body was perfect; her skin was smooth and soft, and her dark, mysterious eyes penetrated every layer of Lucas's defenses, leaving him at her will. Heather loosened his belt and slid her hands under the elastic band of his underwear, dropping them to his knees. Lucas's dick was hard, only its weight preventing it from pointing straight up. Heather cupped his balls in her right hand and toyed with the head of his dick with her left. To avoid climaxing, Lucas pulled Heather close and pressed his hard dick against her soft, warm stomach and held her tightly, allowing his level of arousal to trail off.

As Lucas pulled his pants and underwear the rest of the way off, he said, "Heather, let's go into the other room."

"What's on your mind, big guy?"

"You're on my mind, that's what."

Lucas pulled off his shirt and tie and tossed them on top of his pants, all piled next to the front door.

Completely disrobed, Heather reached for his dick with her left hand and said, "Follow me; I'm going to give you something to remember." With Lucas in tow she headed for the bedroom.

Upon reaching the bedroom, Heather released his dick and tossed herself onto the middle of the bed. Lying on her right side, with her head resting on her right hand, she patted a spot on the bed right next to her and said, "I want you to lie down right here, relax, and forget your hard day at the office."

Lucas complied and lay down next to Heather on his back. Heather immediately rolled over on top of Lucas and straddled him, with her weight on her knees and lower legs. She maneuvered so that her pubic area rested on Lucas's dick. Then she began to move her buttocks in a circular fashion, increasing Lucas's excitement while kissing him passionately.

Toying with Lucas's emotions, she pulled her lower body toward Lucas's chest while pushing down her hips, allowing her female parts to tease his dick. First she inserted his dick into her wetness, and then she pulled forward, allowing it to drop out. She continued doing this until Lucas couldn't stand the torture any longer. As Heather lowered herself and inserted the head of his dick another time, Lucas, with both hands, reached around for the cheeks of her butt, slid his hands high inside her legs, and pulled her down while spreading her warm, soft lips wide open.

Lucas's dick slid deep into Heather's well-lubricated cavern. Still holding the inside of her legs, he could feel his balls pressing against the backs of his hands, telling him that his dick was completely inside of Heather. Heather lifted her chest and began a motion that stimulated them both to the point of climax. Every muscle in Heather's body stiffened, requiring her to sit up straighter, with her back arched away from Lucas, holding his dick motionless deep inside of her. Sensing Heather's climax, Lucas held Heather tightly as he shifted his thoughts of pleasure back to himself.

Suddenly, he felt a sense of euphoria as his dick exploded as deep into Heather as he could push it. As Heather tightened her muscles, she could feel his dick pulsate with his climax, leaving his own deposit of love juice.

Lying there, limp from emotional exhaustion, Lucas still deep inside of Heather, they both fell asleep.

The alarm went off at ten o'clock, giving Lucas and Heather one hour to get ready. Knowing that they only had an hour, they decided to forgo their desire to continue where they had left off. The thought of being in Indianapolis in a few hours, giving them the evening to themselves without time constraints, made their sacrifice more palatable. Access to only one bathroom made the process a little awkward, but it was nothing a dose of creativity couldn't fix.

"Lucas, why don't you use the bathroom first?" asked Heather. "While you do that, I will pack a few clothes."

"Sounds like a plan," said Lucas. Once in the bathroom Locus looks down at the little general and thinks to himself, *you're in good shape little fellow, so don't let me down. This Heather gal is something else, and it will take everything we have to keep her happy.*

Within an hour, they were off on their trip to see the Indianapolis 500. They stopped briefly at Lucas's apartment, to pick up a few clothes for the overnight trip. From there, their latest adventure began to unfold.

"Heather, you like pie?"

"You bet! Doesn't everyone?"

"Everyone I know. There's a family-style restaurant with homemade pies almost as tall as you. This place is about forty miles east of St. Louis. Wanna stop?"

"Sure."

"Wish I could think of the name of this place, but we will see the billboards once we get close. If you'd like, we can also put the top down when we stop, to soak up a little sun as we head toward Indy. Oh! I just thought of the name; it's Aunt Betty's Café. I always stop there when I can."

"Putting the top down is a good idea; I need a little sun."

Once inside they both enjoyed a piece of banana cream pie and a cup of coffee. Recently for them, dessert had been found in bed, but today things were different: dessert was actually served up on a plate. Like their bedroom desserts, seconds were a must, so they purchased a full fruit pie to take along for later.

With the top down, the red Corvette headed east down Interstate 70. Their hair blew freely as the wind whipped through the car. Both donned aviator sunglasses, light tops, and shorts.

"Next stop: Norton's Inn near the airport!" proclaimed Lucas.

It was nearly six o'clock local time when they reached the hotel. Lucas took care of the room while Heather remained in the car. They were both traveling light, so unpacking wasn't an issue. Once in their room, they only unpacked the few items they'd need in the morning: toiletries and the clothing they planned to wear to the track.

The room was a typical motel room. The combination dressing room/bathroom was immediately to the right of the main door. A king bed stood beyond the bathroom, on the right wall. Six big, fluffy pillows were arranged at the head of the bed. Each side of the bed came with an end table and an attractive lamp. A dresser and TV had been placed across from the bed. An armchair and ottoman sat in one corner. The back wall of the room doubled as a sliding door leading to the pool area. The discovery of a pool came as an unexpected surprise to both Lucas and Heather.

After settling into their room, it was time to explore the area and grab a bite to eat. Within walking distance was a wine shop, where food is limited to snacks; a Burger and Brew, and a Country Kitchen restaurant. After a short deliberation, they made their way to the Country Kitchen for a little down-home cooking. Feeling relaxed and fed, Heather suggested they swing by the wine-and-cheese shop on their way back to the room.

With four bottles of wine and several packages of cheese in tow, they returned to the room. Passing through the lobby, Heather couldn't help but notice all the people lined up at the counter, waiting to check in. Their garb gave them away as race fans, wearing all kinds of fancy shirts and caps emblazoned with their favorite driver's car and number.

Having stored their wine and cheese, Lucas and Heather were ready to kick back and enjoy the evening.

"Heather, why don't we watch just a little local news to get a good feel for the weather tomorrow, and see if we can find something about tomorrow's race? OK with you?"

"Sure. Whatever you want to do."

"Since this is your first trip to the race, I want to make sure we're dressed for the weather. We might even find out something about the race that you'll find interesting."

"Lucas, everything we're doing is interesting. I've heard about the Indy 500 in the past, but never dreamed that I would actually be here someday. Did you notice all the people in the lobby when we came in? Most were wearing Indy garb. Guess they're like us, here for the race?"

"Right, and you'll see hundreds of thousands more like them tomorrow. I think you'll love the race, and the excitement of being with all those people."

"Do you have a special shirt or something to wear?" Heather asked. "Since you've been here so many times?"

"The only thing I wear nowadays is my Indy cap. I learned a long time ago that you never know what to wear until the night before, so I always pack light—that includes these long-sleeved Florida shirts," he explained, holding one up. "That probably isn't their real name, but they're worn in hot climates to protect your skin from the sun. I've found that they also keep me warm when it's a little chilly. Never know what to expect in Indianapolis in late May."

"I'm going to feel out of place tomorrow without any Indy clothes."

"Don't worry, Heather; you're in good hands. We'll pick something up for you tomorrow. Something that will help you fit right in."

"Good, because I want to fit in. What time are we getting up?"

"Probably around six; you know that will be five our time."

"That's early."

"It is, but it'll give us enough time to throw some clothes on, get a bite to eat, and be just a little ahead of the crowd. The track is only about twenty minutes from here."

"You know best. You have the experience. Whatever and whenever you want to do something is fine by me."

"Even that early, we'll still encounter traffic near the track. Heather, you up for sampling one of the bottles of wine we bought?"

"Sure am! I was afraid you were going to take them back with us."

"You know, I've been thinking about that pie since we left the restaurant. While I get the wine, Heather, why don't you cut us a piece of pie? I asked the lady to include some paper plates and plastic utensils. They should be in the box."

"I can handle that. What time does the race start?"

"You know, I have to check my ticket every year, but I think it gets underway at noon. Did you bring a swimsuit?"

"No, should I have? I didn't think of it."

"I guess not. I never do, but with our room opening onto to the pool, it seems like a fun thing to do."

"Do we need a suit?" Heather asked.

"The night before the 500, Indianapolis turns into a party town. There's likely to be a large number of people around the pool until late. If we were to go skinny dipping, it would have to be even later because of the crowd. I don't see that happening. In the past, this motel has always been quiet and orderly. That's one thing I like about this place and why I keep coming back."

"I know it would be late, but if you want to go swimming I have a sports bra and my running shorts. I could wear that. Do you have something?"

"Guess I could wear these shorts. The only other shorts I have, I may need tomorrow if I don't wear my jeans. Tell you what Heather: why don't we just enjoy our wine and cheese and see what the pool looks like later?"

"Sounds good to me," replied Heather.

The evening slipped away from Heather and Lucas. Soon it was eleven, and the time had passed so quickly they felt like they'd just arrived. Both sat on the floor with wine and cheese within arm's reach.

"Heather, we managed to kill one bottle of wine and about a pound of cheese, not to mention half a blackberry pie. What do you say we get ready for bed?"

"You want to go first? Would you prefer I go?" asked Heather.

"My dear, why don't you go and I'll guard the next bottle of wine?"

"Sure you will! You'll probably have it half-consumed by the time I get back!"

"How long will you be?" asked Lucas.

"Think you're going to miss me, huh?"

"I already miss you, but I'm just wondering how much time I will have by myself with the wine."

"Aren't you just special?" she asked as she put a hand on each side of his face, scrunched up her nose, and playfully rubbed their noses together. "I won't be gone long; I just want to take a shower and brush my teeth."

"In that case, I'll save a little wine for you."

"Ha, ha, ha: aren't you funny?"

Shortly after Heather started the shower, she emerged from around the bathroom door and said, "You know, Lucas, this process would go much faster if you relinquished your wine-guarding duties and showered with me. We would be finished in half the time. Also, it probably isn't a big deal, but I don't own a pair of pj's. OK with you if I sleep in my birthday suit?"

As Lucas rose to his feet and set down his glass, he said, "Actually, I was hoping you would. Showering together?" Lucas asked. "This will be a first for me." *Bet I know what Heather wants, and I bet I have it!*

"Cool!" Heather disappeared into the bathroom and into the shower.

"OK, Heather, what end do I get? The shower end or the cold end?"

"Whichever end you want; just climb in. Hope you like a hot shower."

"Normally I do, but I sense that if we are to going to successfully wash ourselves, I may need a cold one." *I honestly think she looks better every time I see her, and I really don't think she has a clue how beautiful, how sexy she is.*

"Cut it out and get in here. Tell you what. I'll make showering easy for you. You can skip the cold water tonight. You stand under the water with your back to me. Adjust the water temperature so you're comfortable."

Heather used the liquid soap provided by the motel to lather up. Pouring soap into both hands, she coated her chest and then reloaded both hands with more soap. Nudging up to Lucas, she reached around and began washing his chest and stomach. Replenishing the soap, she began to wash his cock, with strokes from its head to his balls. Heather couldn't help but think to herself, *geez he feels good, rock solid, this guy turns me on big time.*

"Don't even ask," she said. "I'm not jerking you off; I'm washing you."

"Well, you're doing a fine job, but that isn't how I do it. For one thing, my dick isn't usually pointing to the ceiling."

"Just relax."

"Relax? With you pulling on my dick?"

Heather continued to wash Lucas's back with her chest, and his front with her hands, but it didn't take long before she also lost all interest in a shower.

"OK, Lucas," she said. "Your turn to wash me. Let's switch positions."

Lucas and Heather carefully maneuvered around so that Heather was under the shower and Lucas had soap duty. Lucas lathered his chest and tummy and moved close to Heather.

"Heather, this isn't going to work. With the little general in his current state, I can't get close enough." Lucas's dick stood tall and hard.

"Well, use your imagination. Get close and I'll help."

Reaching down between her legs, she pulled the little general down and put it between her legs, then squeezed gently. The head of Lucas's cock rubbed against her most sensitive part without effort on Lucas's part.

Soap in both hands, he began washing her breasts and stomach. He moved down to her pubic area, but his own cock protruded through her legs, making it difficult to be as thorough as he wanted. The cleaner she got, the more excited they both got.

"Heather, this isn't going to work," he said in a frustrated tone." Let's get the soap off both of us and do this right. Turn around. I want to inspect my handiwork."

"Sure you do. You don't want to inspect anything. You just want to put it in."

Now face to face, the little general pressed hard against Heather's stomach. Heather and Lucas hugged and kissed as the water streamed over the two of them. Neither cared about a shower. They both began to breathe heavily. Their bodies were sensitive, even to the force of the water—much less one another's touch.

"Let's make a little adjustment, Heather. I'm going to hold the little general down, and you lift your right leg just a little."

Lucas reached around to Heather's right buttock and gently lifted her, allowing his cock to gently enter her. She could feel her insides fill with the pleasure of Lucas's enormous dick. Her indescribable euphoric sense was overpowering.

"Lucas, let's make a dash for the bed. I want to fuck you until you beg for mercy."

Once towel-dried, they both made tracks to the bed, their private launching pad for their next adventure into each other.

The alarm went off at five. Without hesitation, Lucas and Heather both rose.

"Heather, you can use the restroom first," Lucas said. "I'll make us coffee."

"Got it."

With that, Heather grabbed her overnight case and headed for the bathroom while Lucas made a small pot of coffee. Lucas delivered Heather's coffee while she tended to her hair. Shortly after that, she emerged from the bathroom and announced that it was Lucas's turn. Their entire bathroom routine took thirty minutes, followed by a quick packing of their bags. Hand-in-hand, each with their own small bag, they headed for the car. In need of a quick breakfast, they headed to Country Kitchen again and then got back in the Corvette for a short trip to the track.

"As we approach Speedway," Lucas said, "the town where the track is located, you'll notice how the traffic gets heavier, even this early in the morning."

"And the race starts at eleven?" Heather asked.

"Noon here in Indy, eleven our time, but there are four or five hundred thousand people attending this race, and it creates a huge traffic nightmare the closer you get to race time."

"I can see the traffic is already building," said Heather.

"See that traffic backup at that exit? What do you think? Is that line of traffic about a mile long? And this is nearly four hours before the race. That exit will take you directly to the track in Speedway."

As Lucas moved over to an open lane, Heather asked, "Why aren't we taking that exit?"

"I can't stand to sit in traffic. We're going north about four miles and then coming down to the track from the north. There's a high school that sells parking spots. That's where we're headed. It's a nice, level, paved lot, and they even open the building so race fans can use their restrooms."

"That's nice of them. How far is the track from the school?"

"About two miles—a nice, healthy walk."

It was a beautiful day in Indianapolis. The sky was bright blue, without a cloud in sight. The temperature was in the upper sixties. The only things visible in the sky were low-flying helicopters for traffic control and other light planes towing banners. The forecast predicted that it would remain clear all day. The temperature was expected to be in the upper seventies or low eighties, making a perfect day for outdoor activities, caps, and sunscreen.

Approaching his preferred exit, Lucas said, "We're here. Well not exactly at the track, but our parking lot is about three miles from here. See how the traffic is backing up?"

"Cars are everywhere; looks like they're all headed in the same direction."

"Mostly they are, but traffic control is exceptional here in Indy. This is a lot of traffic, but it will move right along. Before the race, they turn all of the streets near the track into one-way streets headed toward the track. After the race, they're one-way streets headed *away* from the track."

"I've been noticing license plates from all over the country."

"Not surprised; this is the largest event of its type in the world."

"Mister Lucas, OK if I turn the heater down? Creeping along warms it up in here."

"Go for it; do whatever you need to do to stay comfortable. We're going to turn right at the next light, and our lot is about a mile or two down the road."

"Will the car be safe on the lot?"

"I think so. I've never heard of anyone having a problem. The school may even have someone on duty during the race, I've just never asked the question."

"Lucas, I just want to mention that last night was fun. Thanks for bringing me."

Putting his arm around Heather's shoulder, Lucas replied, "I'm glad you came. You're changing this annual pilgrimage for the better. Makes me wonder why we didn't do this last year."

"Can't worry about what we didn't do, Lucas. Let's just enjoy what we have now."

"Sounds good to me," replied Lucas. Pointing toward the high school, Lucas said, "There's the school. That's where we're headed. We'll park the car here and then walk about two miles to the track. Think you're up to it?"

"After last night, I could walk ten miles." *Actually my business is sore, and I would prefer not walking, but I can take it.*

Lucas leaned over and kissed Heather on the head without saying anything.

Then Lucas pulled his money clip from his pocket and gave it to Heather, asking her to peel twenty dollars off the top to pay for parking.

One of the high school students greeted Lucas and Heather and collected the parking fee as they pulled into the lot. Lucas parked his shiny, red Corvette in an area that looked as well-protected from door dings as possible, considering the event. Heather and Lucas put the top up and secured the car. Once that task was completed, they pulled a backpack from the trunk that they'd already stocked with a supply of water, sunscreen, binoculars, and two radios to provide hearing protection and help them stay informed about the event. Prior to beginning their hike to the track, they both used the school's restrooms. Before heading in different directions, they agreed to meet at the front door.

"I know that a two-mile hike is a little much, but I think this is the best place to park," Lucas said when they met up again. "I've been doing this for years. I think you will even find the walk to the track interesting." *I hadn't ever been concerned about my car in the past, but with Heather bringing it up, it makes me wonder.*

"Well, I sure am looking forward to it. I just can't believe this atmosphere! So many people for one event!"

"Mind-boggling, isn't it?"

Lucas and Heather began their journey. Lucas wore the back-pack and Heather walked empty-handed. Everything she would need was either in the backpack or in her pockets. Lucas wore jeans to protect his legs from the afternoon sun, and to provide warmth from the early morning chill he'd sometimes encountered at this event. His shirt was a light blue, long-sleeved shirt, also for warmth and for protection from the sun. Should it be necessary, the sleeves could always be rolled up. Since the sun had never bothered her before and she wanted to dress for afternoon heat, Heather wore Bermuda shorts and a light tan, strapless top. Both wore running shoes.

The walk to the track, Lucas said, would take about forty minutes. There were two routes to choose from. One was on concrete for the entire trip, and the other cut through a huge field also used for camping. Walking through the grass was the shorter of the two, but not always the cleanest, and definitely not the smoothest. They opted for the longer, smoother route on the way to the track, but planned to use the shortcut after the race. Along the way they passed a church that also sold parking spaces.

By then, the track was in sight. Its massive structure on the north end of the track made it seem closer than it actually was. The street that ran next to the sidewalk they used had been turned into a one-way street. There were cars and buses lined up two abreast, creeping along. Those cars made up a line of traffic about a mile long, headed for an enormous grass field used to park cars and operated by the track. Strolling along at a comfortable pace, Heather and Lucas enjoyed the sights, especially the people, along the way.

All the nearby homes had turned their lawns into parking lots. The closer to the track they were, the more expensive those manicured parking spots became. Out by the school, a parking spot cost ten dollars, while a home within blocks of the track might sell a spot for as much as forty dollars. Many of those same one-day entrepreneurs also sold ice water and soda, and the really aggressive homeowners even included hot dogs and other food. Official vendors began to pop up about a quarter of a mile from the track, selling everything from T-shirts to radios and toy cars. If you could name it, they probably sold it.

On the north end of the track was a large, grassy area. Only about one-quarter of that area got early morning shade, so race fans tended to gather close to the track to get a little rest and avoid the sun before finding their seats. Finding seats for the regular fans was not an issue, but for the first-timer it could be like looking for a needle in a haystack. The track was a two-and-a-half-mile oval with bleachers lining most of the track, except for the back stretch and portions of the curves. Finding your assigned seat could be tricky.

Heather and Lucas entered the track at the north end and made their way to the grassy area and shade. While Heather staked their claim on a small piece of turf, Lucas went to the closest concession stand for two cups of coffee. After returning to Heather, they both stretched out and engaged in people watching.

"OK, buster: watch it," Heather said while looking at Lucas as a young, tall blond strolled by.

"You like her choice of clothing today, Heather? A halter top two sizes too small and shorts she no doubt had to lie on a bed to zip up."

"Shorts? Those aren't shorts! I can see her checks and everything else," Heather responded. "What's the deal? You have that look in your eye, Mr. Lucas. Like to get into those shorts?"

"Not interested," Lucas said. "I'm already with the most beautiful woman here."

"Sure," Heather replied. "I don't think you're horny, so it must be the sun."

"Check this guy out, Heather."

A middle-aged fellow walked by. He was built like a Coke bottle, wearing biker garb, and had a mustache at least nine inches on each side.

"You will see anything and everything today," Said Lucas.

With disbelief in her voice, Heather asked Lucas if he thought another approaching lady realized that people could see right through her skirt.

"Heather, that's why she's wearing it. She wants the attention. Sad part is, she's a looker and doesn't need to flaunt her stuff. Just the same, I'll let you know what I can see." *Well, I can see everything, but after last night, sex is the last thing on my mind.*

Heather swatted Lucas across the shoulder in a flirtatious way, clearly not intending to inflict pain.

"Hey, I'm not looking at anything she isn't showing me. Anyway, like I already said, you are the most beautiful, sexy woman here. If there weren't so many people around, I'd show you what an effect you have on me." Lucas reflected on his own statement, thinking to himself, *I know I said it light hearted, but I really do believe that Heather is the most beautiful lady I have ever met.*

Heather scooted closer to Lucas and hugged his left arm, resting her head lightly on his shoulder.

"Lucas, I hope you know you're special to me. Tell me more about yourself. Your parents—you never mention them."

"They passed away five years ago."

"Sorry to hear that; I didn't know."

"I understand. It's about ten; want to start walking toward our seats?"

"I'll follow you, Mister Lucas, to our seats and beyond."

"OK," said Lucas with a chuckle.

Lucas slung his backpack into position and, after a quick tug on the straps, was ready to continue the pilgrimage to their seats. Each carrying an unfinished cup of coffee, they headed south along the perimeter of the track.

Not wanting the conversation to shift from Lucas, Heather continued to ask probing questions.

"Do you have any brothers or sisters?"

"I had a brother; he passed away about three years ago."

"I don't know what to say. I am truly sorry for asking."

"That's OK. You didn't know. Besides, it's not a secret. He wasn't well. He drank and smoked too much for years. It finally got the best of him."

"Was he older than you?"

"Yes, by about fifteen years, but still too young to die."

"Wow."

Lucas and Heather continued walking toward their seats, enjoying the crowd along the way. As a game, Lucas suggested they see who could spot the most movie stars, recording artists, or other public figures. The crowd was very heavy, and it didn't take long to figure out that the probability of seeing a famous person was remote. They concluded that any notable people were probably already in their rooms overlooking the track, or wherever people like that went during the race.

"Heather, I told you I would buy you a T-shirt or whatever. Let's stop at this concession stand and see what they have that turns your crank."

"Oh, good! I want to look like I fit in."

"My dear, you would fit in wherever you go, whatever you wear. Even so, if you can't find something in here you like, you won't find it anywhere."

Both cruised through the official gift shop located beneath the bleachers. The shop was packed, making it difficult to move around.

"Looks like everyone has the same idea: to get something before the race starts," said Lucas.

"Well, I just found the perfect shirt. What do think?" Heather said while holding up the shirt.

"I think it looks nice. It's you." It was a pink T-shirt that read "Indianapolis 500," the numerals outlined in rhinestones. The bling seemed a little much, but Lucas didn't want to criticize her fashion choices.

As they exited the shop, Heather said, "I'll be right back. I'm going to the restroom to change."

When she met up Lucas again, she said, "Well, what do you think?"

"Looks nice! Your shirt sparkles just like your eyes."

"Oh, you're just saying that. Mind if I put my other shirt in the backpack?"

"Not at all." Lucas swung around, making the zipper accessible to Heather.

Pointing to a set of stairs leading to the top of the bleachers, Lucas said, "We need to go up those stairs, all the way to the top. I think you'll like our seats. There're on the top row, so you can stand if you wish, or sit. We'll also be under cover, so the sun won't roast us—and there's usually a breeze, so it's a little cooler than other seats."

After reaching the top row of seats, Lucas and Heather began to settle in for the day. The seats were on the aisle, so reaching their seats and stowing the backpack were extremely easy. Both began the process of readying themselves for the race. Lucas retrieved the radios from the backpack and ensured they had fresh batteries. He kept one and gave the other to Heather. He pulled out the binoculars next. After cleaning the lenses, Lucas hung them around his neck. Bottles of water and sunscreen were carefully set out, to be available to either person in need of them. He kept the granola bars in the backpack until they'd need them.

Heather located the sun screen and began to rub some on her legs, arms, and face. "Look right down here, Heather." Lucas pointed to the pit entrance. "Once the race starts, you'll see a lot of action from here. Several times during the race, every car pulls into the pit area, and at times it becomes very busy—almost dangerous.

"All the way to our right is the fourth-turn exit, and to the far left is the entrance to the first turn. This place is so big, you can't see the entire track from any one seat."

"What's all that activity down on the track?" Heather asked.

"Those are the thirty-three cars on the starting grid. They were staged there a little while ago. Once we get within a few minutes of starting the race, the drivers will get in their cars and start their engines. Once that happens, we'll need to put our earplugs in. It's too loud without them. We'll also want to put our radios on to monitor the race; they will also help reduce the noise."

In the meantime, Heather remained in awe of the festivities, the thousands of people, the enormity of the track, and the event in general. She watched and listened to the prayer being spoken over the loudspeaker, the playing of taps, the singing of the national anthem, and 'Back Home Again in Indiana," a crowd favorite by Jim Nabors. Then those famous words came over the speakers: "Ladies and gentlemen, start your engines!" Following that announcement, engines roared as the event actually got underway.

"OK, Heather, time to put the plugs in. I want you to be very sensitive to the speeds. The first lap will take about two and a half minutes. Know how long that feels: two and a half minutes, just waiting for anything. The next parade lap is made in about two minutes. Once the race starts, the trip around the track will take somewhere around forty seconds, and the cars fly by so fast you can hardly tell them apart. They're loud: when a group goes by, you can't hear anything, but the roar of engines."

Listening intently, Heather's eyes get bigger in disbelief about what she is about to witness. Stretching to see the fourth turn, she can see the pace car exiting the turn in front and the thirty-three cars strung out behind. Heather couldn't decide whether she was scared or just excited, but she felt something that put her body on edge.

Lucas got right next to Heather's right ear and said, "Hold on. The next time they come around, the race will start, and when they get on the gas, you'll see it, hear it, and feel it. It always scares me—makes me nervous on the inside to see that many cars traveling over two hundred miles per hour and so close to one another."

Heather couldn't see the cars, but she heard the announcer in her radio say that the green flag had dropped, and that the race was underway. She was still processing those words when she saw the large group of cars come out of turn four as though they'd been shot out of a cannon. They flew by her vantage point in a blur. Her heart raced as car after car flew down the straightaway and disappeared into turn one. No sooner were they out of sight than the lead pack once again came out of turn four, all of them moving so fast she could hardly tell who was in front. She wondered whether she could take the stress—or excitement, or whatever emotion she felt—for the duration of the race.

The pack of cars passing in front of Heather was so loud it was impossible to hear anything being broadcast through her ear-muff radio. The noise was so intense that it even interfered with her ability to think and process what was happening.

Accompanying the thunderous noise was a vibration that passed through her body as the shock waves reached the stands. The vibrations seemed to be in constant pursuit of the roaring engines causing them. Each car passing by at more than 225 miles per hour could be heard and felt, but hardly seen. Knowing the cars were being driven by people risking their lives created an unexpected, mystical sexual arousal in Heather. Though she'd never considered herself to be a racing enthusiast, she'd begun to understand the attraction as her body awakened to new sensations.

Once the race settled down and the cars spread out a little, Heather and Lucas also settled down. Lap after lap, they watched as the leaders became apparent and strategy played out. After 200 laps of pure excitement, Heather could say she had seen her first Indy 500.

Immediately following the race, Heather and Lucas joined the hundreds of thousands of fans beginning their exodus. Making their way back to the car, they both walked briskly. Neither understood why they walked so fast, since they still had a five-hour drive ahead. Nevertheless, they forged on at a rapid pace.

When they reached the car, they tossed the backpack into the trunk and retrieved fresh bottles of water. They dropped the top to enjoy the beautiful day, and let the car's air conditioner provide a cool breeze.

Getting out of the parking lot wasn't difficult, since the traffic moved slowly and there was always a kind motorist willing to let cars merge from the lots into the flow of traffic. As they moved away from the track, the pace picked up. All lanes, as Lucas had said, flowed one way to handle the enormous crowd. Within fifteen minutes, Heather and Lucas reached the interstate and accelerated to highway speeds.

"Heather, you hungry?"

"A little."

"Let's go as far as Terre Haute and see if we can find a place to eat there."

"Sounds like a plan. I still want to know more about you. You're one big mystery."

"Big, am I? Is that what you think, Heather?"

"Well, not like that. Actually, when I think about it, you *are* sometimes."

"OK, potty mouth."

"Seriously, I don't know anything about you."

"You know everything about me," replied Lucas.

"I don't know what your childhood was like."

"Why do you care about that?" *Heather is a neat young lady, but what's with all her questions about my past. They're beginning to piss me off.*

"I don't necessarily, but you said I know everything and I don't."

"Let's change the subject and talk about something fun, like where we're going next. Ever been to San Antonio?"

"No, but I hear it's beautiful—a fun place to go. Are we going to San Antonio?" *Wow! At first I couldn't get Lucas to give me the time of day, and now we're making weekend trips and fucking like rabbits. Wonder what's next!*

"Perhaps. Let's see what's going on over the next few weeks." *San Antonio is one of my most favorite cities in the country. I would love to introduce the city, the river walk and all the fun places to Heather. She would love to sit on the Riverwalk and just watch the people. Maybe we can do it.*

En route to St. Louis, Lucas and Heather stopped for a quick bite to eat in Terre Haute. Once both stomachs and the car's gas tank were filled, they continued to head west. By then, the sun was low in the horizon, with a beautiful sunset in red and gold. The warm wind whipped through their hair as they sat silently, enjoying the passing landscape and the comfort that came from being so close to one another. Both were mesmerized as the sun inched its way below the horizon, until it seemed to give in to the night sky.

As Heather watched the sun disappear, she thought about how much she'd enjoyed the trip, and about how much she hated to see the day melt away. With each passing mile, the day and their adventure came that much closer to ending.

"Lucas, I don't want this day to end!"

"Heather, there can't be another day if this one doesn't end," responded Lucas in an upbeat tone.

"I know, but this has been a special weekend. Had I not gone with you to Indy, I probably would've been invited over to one of my girlfriends' houses and spent the day there. Sad part is, I'd never have known what I was missing."

"Stop thinking about what might have been and think about what you did, or what you are going to do tomorrow."

"You sound like a psychologist."

"Well, it *is* my major, but that's not where I'm coming from. I just think people should always think about where there're going, not so much about where they've been."

"See, that's the kind of stuff about you that I don't know. Where do you come up with these thoughts?"

"It would be impossible for us to sit holding hands and looking into each other's eyes while I told you everything on my mind, or how I think. That stuff just takes time. Be patient; in time you will know me better than I know myself."

"If you say so. Do you fly tomorrow?"

"No."

"Want to spend the night?"

"I shouldn't. I need to get up early and do some serious studying. You know it won't be long until I'm out of school. Speaking of which, this summer school stuff sucks."

"You'll like that—the airline job and extra time on your hands. Think I will see you when you get out of school?"

"Why wouldn't you?"

"You're going to go into the flight-training program for Global, and who knows where you'll be based? I won't see you at the airport anymore."

"Will you knock it off, Heather? We'll continue seeing each other all the time."

"Promise?"

"Yes, I promise."

With that reassurance, Heather leaned over to Lucas and placed her head on his right shoulder and her right hand on the inside of his right leg. The hum of the engine and the constant, steady noise of the wind created a warm and comfortable setting in the dim evening light. Heather gently rubbed Lucas's leg in both a soothing and stimulating way. Before long, she could feel the head of his cock against her hand. Very gently, she stroked it through his pants.

"What's going on, Mr. Lucas? What's on your mind?"

"I guess about the same thing you're thinking. Your fault, you know."

"How's that?"

"I'm sitting here minding my own business, just cruising along, and you start playing with me." *Wonder if I could pull off the road for a quickie?*

"I wasn't playing with you." She looked up at him. "I was just rubbing your leg."

"Where do you think my leg is located? That's my dick you're rubbing."

"Well, it wasn't there when I started."

"That's a shocker. Wonder what caused that?"

"I think the little general is trying to escape. Let me help!" She unzipped his pants.

"What the hell are you doing? "

"You focus on your driving; I'll take care of the general. I'm just trying to release him from bondage.

Heather carefully maneuvered the little general to be completely exposed, hard as a rock and held erect by Heather's right hand.

"There. That has to feel better. Free at last. Good thing it's dark now. Mr. Lucas, can you slide the seat back just a little?"

"I can, but I'm not sure I should."

"Go for it, big guy."

With the aid of his power seat, Lucas moves the seat back slightly and asked, "How's that?"

"You tell me." Heather bent down and put his dick into her mouth.

"What the fuck? Are you kidding me? Oh my God!" *Focus on the road*, Lucas said to himself.

Heather began gently moving up and down, occasionally licking the head of his dick as though it were an ice cream bar on a stick. She then returned to a slow, steady up-and-down motion, using her tongue to embrace the upper extension his cock.

Feeling Lucas's dick in her mouth brought Heather close to a climax. As her own excitement grew, Heather began sucking the swollen head of his dick. She could feel his dick start to throb as her own heart rate quickened. Lifting her head slightly, with her right hand on the lower part of his dick to hold it in place, Heather could pull back and examine the little general up close. *Gee, I've never really looked at a dick so closely,* she thought. *It really is neat. How can something that is usually just hanging around, being tucked away in underwear or a swimsuit, grow so large and hard? It's hard, but still soft to the touch, and it has this neat little helmet with one eye. I think I love you, little general. I'm one lucky gal.*

Having had a good look at the dick that had caused such pleasure in her recent past, Heather returned to the task at hand: giving Lucas a thrill to remember. Holding his dick with her right hand, she once again began to suck hard on the little general.

Lucas's dick was almost totally consumed by Heather's mouth, with her tongue swirling from its little helmet to its base, just above his balls. Such stimulation caused Lucas to feel a climax approaching.

"Heather, if you don't stop I'm going to come. Oh my God. Oh, this is crazy fucking stuff we're doing here. I think I love it. If I could get to your stuff, I'd eat you alive."

Heather continued to suck on the head of Lucas's dick when she climaxed without warning. Heather spread her legs and reached down with her right hand to press hard against her wet panties, trying to help contain the surge of emotional energy rushing through her body. Not losing her focus on the dick in her mouth, she continued to use her tongue to massage the head as she slowly and deliberately moved up and down.

Lucas could sense Heather's climax, and her tongue was no match for his willpower. Out of control, Lucas also climaxed with a shock wave passing through his body. The only thing keeping Lucas from losing control of his body with each euphoric surge was his need to drive the car. Every other muscle was frozen by his electrifying discharge.

Heather could feel and taste Lucas's eruption as his climax peaked and his dick throbbed uncontrollably. Feeling Lucas's climax caused Heather to experience another climax herself. Still holding her wet panties, she could feel her muscles contracting as she pushed hard to contain herself.

Once they both began to regain control of themselves, Heather kissed his cock's throbbing head before she tucked it away. She carefully zipped his pants up before patting the little general on his head.

Resting her head on Lucas's right breast, she asked, "Do you think we can do this again sometime? If so, sometime can't come soon enough."

"Heather, you are one fucking surprise after another. I can't spend the night, but I have a special night planned for you in the near future."

"You always do."

# CHAPTER NINE
## *Trip to the Lake*

❦

As Lucas approached his front door a few days later, he heard the phone ringing inside. Since he seldom received calls on his home line from anyone except work or school, he automatically assumed it would be an important call and made a dash for the phone. En route to the ringing phone, he chastised himself for not having an answering machine.

Snatching the phone from the cradle, Lucas hurriedly said, "Hello? Hello? Are you there?"

After a few seconds of silence, he heard a voice say, "Hello? Lucas, is that you?"

"Yes, who is this?"

"This is Frank Morrison from Global. How are you today?"

"Oh, I'm fine, just a little out of breath. I was just coming in when I heard the phone ring. How are you?"

"I'm fine. The last time we talked, I said I would bring you back for a follow-up interview. Are you available one week from today?"

"I will make myself available. How much time should I plan on taking?"

"We'll get a ticket for you on the early flight down, and we can get you back out that afternoon. Lucas, I'll send you an email with the trip details. By then we should have your background check completed, and it looks like we can probably keep your original start date."

"Fantastic! Do you need me to bring anything?"

"No, this interview is just to see whether we can fit you into that next class and the background check is routine. Although we already did one, we always do another one when considering a change in start date. Any questions for now?"

"No, I don't think so. I'll be looking forward to seeing your email and visiting with you next Wednesday. In the meantime, take care and I'll see you soon."

"Have a good week, Lucas. We'll see you Wednesday. If anything comes up, give me a call."

Thursday, just prior to a flight, Lucas made his way to the lobby, following his romantic thoughts. He was on a mission. As he entered the lobby he found Heather busy behind the counter. Her work had obviously captured her attention. With her distracted, Lucas was able to approach the counter unnoticed. Even just standing there, he was taken by her beauty, her charm, and her hair with every strand perfectly in place. Even when just working, she would be sexy and inviting to any guy who wasn't on his death bed . . . and maybe even if he was.

Entertained by watching Heather being Heather, Lucas stood there, quietly capturing her every movement to be recalled at a later date.

Finally unable to resist the urge to steal her attention away from her work, Lucas said in a soft voice, "Heather, you're stunning."

She immediately swung around, got up, and leaned over the counter to give Lucas a quick kiss on the lips.

"Getting ready for tonight's flight?"

"Actually, I'm finished with the preflight. I saw one of the mechanics on the ramp when I pulled in and wanted to ask him a question about the plane's routine maintenance, so I didn't come through the lobby."

"So you weren't trying to avoid me?"

"No way. In fact, I was thinking about our trip to Indy. I had so much fun I wanted to know if you would like to go to the lake with me this weekend. We could leave Friday night when you get off work, and come back Saturday afternoon. I am on standby Sunday, so I need to be in the area. What do you think?"

"Of course I'll go! I would love to go."

"Great. I'll be back late tonight, so why don't I give you a call in the morning and we'll work out the details? While I'm thinking of it, Global called me yesterday and invited me back to Dallas next Wednesday. That was a welcome phone call. I was beginning to worry."

"Lucas, you don't have anything to worry about. You have a good flight tonight, and I'll be waiting for your call in the morning. Every minute will seem like an hour!"

"Heather, you're a mess, you know that?" as Lucas smiled while shaking his head back and forth in disbelief.

"I'm not a mess; I'm horny."

"Well, you just stay that way and I'll see if I can't relieve you soon."

Having established a rough plan for the weekend, they gave each other a quick kiss. Lucas disappeared through the hangar door and Heather returned to her work.

Seeing Lucas made it difficult for Heather to keep her mind on her work. She kept remembering the magic that surrounded the weekend in Indy. She wondered how this weekend could possibly measure up to Indy. Not knowing what to expect at the lake, she allowed her imagination to dominate her thoughts. The more she thought about another trip, the more she neglected her work and let the anticipation heighten her excitement.

Anxious to have a fun, relaxing weekend, Heather decided to call Autumn and ask if she might be able to come in early the next night. If she agreed, Lucas and Heather could get an earlier start. Autumn always appeared to be rather independent, but definitely friendly. Heather remembered Autumn asking about how she and Lucas were getting along. And just a few weeks ago, Heather had covered an entire shift for Autumn. Autumn never told Heather why she needed off, but Heather assumed a guy had something to do with it. Autumn was in her early thirties and active in the dating scene. A night off and a guy seemed to go together.

Heather had second thoughts about calling Autumn. After a short deliberation, Heather decided that it would be more difficult for Autumn to say no if they were face to face. Heather returned to her duties and tried to focus on her job, but was anxious about asking Autumn to cover for her.

The closer it got to the end of her shift, the more anxious she became, until she gave up trying to do anything useful altogether. Instead, she found herself rehearsing what she would say to Autumn. Autumn was as dependable as the rising sun, but seldom got to work before necessary. The clock on the wall told Heather that her shift was about to end. That meant that Autumn would pull into the parking lot any minute.

As Heather's anxiety built, she saw Autumn pull into one of the visitor's parking spots with two minutes to spare. Parking in the visitors' spots was encouraged for the night shift.

Without delay, Autumn headed for the lobby with her signature cup of coffee in one hand and book in the other. After midnight, activity almost came to a halt, so reading a novel was not unusual, especially for Autumn. Had things worked out differently in school, Autumn would have been a writer. Instead, at her parents' insistence, she majored in music. Now she worked overnight hours as a customer service rep at Gold Coast Aviation and gave music lessons to aspiring artists during her free time. When first entering school, she thought music would provide her with an outlet for her creativity, but that didn't happen. After graduating, Autumn resorted to reading the work of others while working at a dead-end job.

Heather recalled Autumn once asking whether life would ever get better. Unfortunately, though Autumn asked the question, she seldom did anything about it. Heather wanted to learn from Autumn's experiences. She wanted to make sure that by the time she reached thirty, she would have a firm grip on where she was going.

As Autumn approached the counter, Heather jumped to her feet and, with an enthusiastic voice, said, "Hey, Autumn; I've got a favor to ask of you."

"What's that, Heather?"

"I have a chance to go to the lake with Lucas tomorrow night and would like to get off to an early start. Think you could pick up the last four hours of my shift?"

"Lucas the pilot? What lake are you going to?"

"Yes, the State Side pilot, but I don't know what lake; he didn't say and I didn't ask."

"It doesn't matter. I owe you from when you covered for me a month or so ago. I'll be happy to take it. Lord knows I don't have anything better to do. I didn't know you and Lucas had a thing going."

"I guess you could call it a thing. He was a tough nut to crack, but once cracked he seems to be a hot number."

"Is that right? So you two get it on?"

"Yeah, but your look: your tone—are you interested in Lucas?"

"Heather, don't be silly. I thought I might've had a chance with him once, but he made it clear that a relationship wasn't in his future." *Hearing Heather talk this way brings out the competitive spirit in me. I don't like hearing some other gal getting a guy that I may have a chance with.*

"I know. I guess I pushed until he caved. Anyway, you were talking about the time I covered for you. I assume you had a hot date that weekend."

"That's right. I thought it was going to be a hot date, but it cooled off quickly."

"So what's the deal, Autumn?" Heather asked. "You sound down tonight."

"I'm just tired of the same old stuff. I'm in a rut: lousy job, no excitement, no romance in my life, just one boring date after another. I already know what next year will look like. It's depressing."

"What will next year look like, and how do you know it?"

"Because I'm living my future. Tomorrow will look like yesterday. Day after day, they're all the same."

"Autumn, why don't you put a plan together for your future?"

"I would, but I don't know what I want it to look like. I don't know what I want to do."

"That's too bad, because if you don't know what it will look like, you won't recognize it if you find it."

"I know, but I wouldn't know how to start planning a future. I just wait for tomorrow to show up and then I deal with it."

"Start tonight. I know it's slow around here after midnight, so rather than reading a book, I want you to sit quietly and ask yourself what will make you happy. What would cause you to want to get up in the morning? Think about this stuff and let me know what you come up with."

"All right," Autumn said, sounding exhausted. "It can't hurt anything."

Autumn and Heather bade one another farewell. Heather didn't waste any time getting home to prepare for a romantic overnight with Lucas. Autumn, on the other hand, was stuck at work trying to define what she wanted her life to look like. *What a daunting task,* she thought. *How many other people are in the same situation? How many are ever successful?* She'd already thought about such questions a million times, and had never been able to come to a conclusion. She thought that maybe she didn't know what made her happy because she'd never experienced it. *Heather is expecting me to do something and will want to talk about what I discovered, so I had better do something.*

Heather reflected on her conversation with Autumn, and knowing that she had no right to give anyone advice on planning a future. She was in a similar situation, after all. The difference between them was that Autumn allowed her situation to get her down while Heather simply dealt with it.

The minute Heather got home, she called Lucas and left a message on his new answering machine, letting him know that she would get off work around six and asking if she should meet him at his apartment or wait for him to swing by her place.

Lucas returned from his trip and immediately went to bed without setting an alarm. He began to join the conscious world around eleven in the morning. Once awake, he lay there in bed until every ounce of energy was restored and the only logical thing to do was to get up and begin the process of creating another day.

Following his morning routine, he cleaned the apartment, did a load of laundry, and went to the grocery store. With all of his responsibilities completed, his attention turned to Heather and the weekend. At three in the afternoon he decided to call Heather to finalize their weekend plans. With a phone in one hand and a cup of coffee in the other, he called Heather.

"Gold Coast Aviation, how may I help you?"

"You can start by having dinner with me tonight."

"Lucas, I was hoping for more than dinner."

"Apparently you missed the word *start*. Anyway, I'll see what I can do about that. I got your message. Can I pick you up at your apartment? When we return, you will probably prefer not to mess with picking up your car. What do you think?"

"I agree. Come Saturday night, I'm sure I'll prefer not to mess with it."

"Settled, my dear. I'll be at your place by the time you get home tonight." *I really wonder how far this relationship is going. I'm having fun now, but long term, I just don't know.*

Just like a finely tuned Swiss watch, Autumn pulled into the parking lot at Gold Coast to relieve Heather at 5:58 p.m.

Although not standing at the door to greet Autumn, Heather was ready to bolt as soon as Autumn reached the lobby. As Autumn stepped into the lobby, Heather began heading for the door.

"Autumn, how you doing tonight?"

"I'm OK. You?"

"I'm looking forward to my weekend with Lucas, that's how I'm doing."

"Bet you are," responded Autumn in a condescending tone.

"Come on, Autumn; don't sound like that. Did you work on that little project last night?"

"Yes, for what good it will do."

"Don't be discouraged if your future doesn't become crystal clear overnight. I want to talk about this more next week, OK? Right now I need to get home."

"We can talk about me if you wish, but I want to hear more about you and Lucas."

"I'm not the kiss-and-tell kind of gal, but you have a good night—and thanks again for helping me out. We'll talk next week. Right?"

"Sure, but if we don't talk about your weekend, it likely won't be a very exciting conversation. Go have fun and don't worry about me."

"Thanks again, Autumn. I owe you."

Having said their good-byes, Heather and Autumn headed in opposite directions.

At a few minutes past six, Heather arrived home and, as advertised, Lucas was waiting patiently in his car with the top down, soaking up the sun. Before Heather could open the door to her own car, Lucas jumped out and pulled it open, extending his right hand to help Heather out. Together, the two grabbed Heather's overnight case from the trunk of her car.

"What do you think, Heather? You ready to head south?"

"Yep! Let's do it."

With that, Lucas put Heather's overnight case into his trunk, helped Heather into the passenger seat, and settled himself into the driver's seat. Both buckled in, and their next adventure got underway.

"Tell me, Lucas, where are we going? I know you said the lake, but I didn't ask which lake and you didn't mention it."

"Sorry about that. We're headed for the Lake of the Ozarks. My plan is to head out Interstate 70 with a pit stop in Fulton. That's about a two-hour run. Sound OK to you?"

"Sounds like a plan. How long will it take us to get to there?"

"Nonstop, it's about a three-hour run, so it just depends on how long we take in Fulton."

"That's not a bad drive. That should put us there around nine thirty or ten. Where are we staying? Do we have reservations?" asked Heather.

"I guess I didn't tell you much about this trip, did I?" he asked.

"Not really."

"Well, we're going to stay on my boat."

"You have a boat?"

"Sure do. It's a beauty. You'll like it."

"I bet. Tell me more!"

"For now, just trust me: you'll like it. We'll be there in a few hours and you can judge for yourself."

"OK, but I have to admit you have my curiosity running in high gear." *This Lucas guy is one giant mystery. He reminds me of Forest Gump and a box of chocolates—you never know what you are going to get. About the time I feel like I know him, he finds a way to convince me that I don't. I would never have guessed we were spending the night on a boat, much less his. This will be another first—sex on a boat!*

It was a beautiful evening. The temperature stayed in the upper seventies with clear skies. The two motored their way to the Lake of the Ozarks, arriving around ten in the evening. Their route took them along Highway 54, across the Bagnell Dam. As they crossed into the "strip," they found traffic congested along a three-mile stretch lined with motels, restaurants, shops, bars, and all sorts of entertainment venues.

Approaching a small grocery store, Lucas announced his plan to stop and buy the supplies needed for their stay. Both went into the store and wandered the aisles, hoping to spot items of interest. Neither was disappointed in their bounty. Though planning to eat most of their meals out, their bags were brimming with snacks and beverages of all kinds. They loaded back into the car and drove a few more miles south.

"Heather," Lucas said, "the marina is just ahead on the right side." Lucas gestured toward the lake. "It's dark, so don't expect to see much. The rows of lights on the docks are pretty much it until daylight. There is the road," Lucas added, pointing to a small, paved road leading down into the marina.

"Wow! This place is nice! These boats are huge! Is yours?"

"No, but it's nice and accommodates my needs."

"How do you do this? Do pilots make that much money?"

"We're paid well. Plus, I'm a good money manager."

"You must be damn good. Think you could manage mine?" *If I had any to manage,* she thought.

Lucas gave another boat owner a friendly gesture without answering Heather. Pointing to a large boat in the last slip on the dock, Lucas said, "That's our home for the evening."

"Damn! How often do you come here?" *These surroundings speak volumes about this place. Without even stepping foot on his boat I am impressed. I don't believe this. Are we on a reality show or something?*

"Not often. I try to make it down about every three weeks or so. This is a quick trip this weekend because I haven't been down for a while and need to run the systems." *This is going to be a new experience for me; having someone on the boat with me, and a looker like Heather. I wonder how this is going to unfold.*

Pointing to a large complex on a hill above the marina, Heather asked, "What is that?"

"It's a combination motel and resort. We're going to put our groceries away, turn the AC on, and then head up the hill and check out the bar while the boat cools down. I like this routine because it gives me an opportunity to settle down. I usually sleep like a baby after a trip to the bar."

"Cool. I can't believe this is your boat, and that I didn't even know you had one, much less one like this!"

"I'm not that comfortable talking about my personal business."

"That's apparent."

With supplies in hand, they both made their way to the dock where the boat was moored. The dock was cordoned off, so Lucas entered his code into the lock, allowing access to the dock. The place had a pleasing, comforting look.

Looking down the dock, one could see land running along the right side and rows of boats on the left. The dock was lit by yellow lights mounted above the walkway every fifty feet, the line of them running the length of the dock. The light was subtle but adequate. The boats were the pride of their owners, and often got more attention than the owners' families and homes. The owners, subsequently, were finicky about visitors and generally didn't like others touching their pride and joy.

Lucas's boat was in the first or last slip, depending on the approach. Entering the last gate, as they had, put his boat directly ahead, making the distance from the car to the boat a short two hundred feet.

Lucas set his grocery bags down and then unzipped the back cover that protected the rear deck of the boat. Once on the boat, he asked Heather to pass her bags to him.

With the groceries on board, Lucas extended a hand to Heather to help her step from the dock onto the back deck of the boat. The rear of the boat had a cushioned seat that ran the width of the boat. A rail ran around the perimeter of the deck. The rail, had a cutout on each side of the boat for getting on and off the boat. A small door led down three steps into the cabin area.

At the bottom of the steps and to the left, Lucas explained, was the "head," a nautical term for bathroom. Opposite the bathroom was a booth capable of seating four people. A small couch and "galley," or kitchen, rounded out the left side of the cabin. All the way to the front of the cabin was a double bed. The walls were decorated to meet the taste of a single guy, which included several airplane pictures. Back on the deck, the controls, steering wheel, radio, and depth finder were elevated on the right side, permitting the captain to have a forward view through an upper windshield, complete with a windshield wiper in case a voyage included rain.

"Heather, let's turn the AC on and then go get the luggage."

"You take the lead and I'll follow," responded Heather. *This is one fucking awesome boat. Air-conditioning, a TV...this is a fucking house that floats.* The two made their way back to the car, grabbed their luggage, and returned to the boat. After unpacking all of the essentials and finishing preparing the cabin, their stay on the lake was ready to begin.

"Ready to go to the bar and indulge in a nightcap?" asked Lucas.

"Sure, I'm with you. Do we need to follow the driveway back to Highway 54, or is there a shortcut?"

"Oh, there's a shortcut. There are steps right behind my car that lead straight to the bar. They make it easy."

"If I owned the bar, I'd make it easy too," responded Heather." *By the look of these boats, I think I'd provide a shuttle.*

Lucas and Heather spent the next couple of hours in the bar, putting distance between themselves and their work as they allowed themselves to be absorbed by an environment designed for fun, relaxation, and romance.

The bar was perched on top of the hill, with large picture windows and a deck. There were two doors that led to an outside seating area on a deck that ran the width of the bar and then wrapped around the sides. The deck provided a romantic view of the lake and marina. The marina sat on the lake, and the only lighting on the dock were the yellow pedestrian lights mounted above the walkway. Because the lights were mounted above the walkway and under the cover of the roof, they were not directly visible from the bar, so the dock took on an ill-defined look from above. In the evening, the atmosphere was very warm and comfortable.

The motel sat on the hill directly above the marina. The hill was steep and mostly covered with pine trees, separating the marina parking lot and the motel. The motel was arranged like a resort, with a variety of activities right on the property, including three bars, a bowling alley, and a theater. All of the rooms had outside access, with yellow lights just outside each door. Like the marina, the motel had an aura of romance at night. The complex was built on multiple levels on the side of the hill, giving it an interesting look.

At around two in the morning, Lucas suggested they return to the boat and turn in. With the bar tab paid, they began their return pilgrimage down the steep, wooden steeps.

"Lucas, I think I'm living a dream. This place is beautiful. I can't believe you only come here every three weeks. If this were my boat, I'd be here every weekend."

"When I'm here, I feel the same way."

"Why don't you come more often?"

"Summer school and other stuff."

"Do you come down by yourself?" Heather asked.

"Usually. Why? Who would I bring, Mike?"

"What about me? I'm available."

"If you recall, we just started seeing each other."

"I know, but I didn't even know you had a boat. This isn't how I see you. I think of you as someone who talks and thinks in hundreds of miles per hour and thousands of feet—someone talking about the city you went to yesterday and the city you're going to tomorrow."

"I understand what you're saying, but this place is different. Listen. What do you hear?"

Heather responded with a crisp, "Nothing."

"Exactly. This place is like heaven on earth! It's my escape; it's where I come and don't need to think about anything. I can just relax, and if I choose to be mentally engaged, I make plans for the future, or whatever. Generally I come down, go to the bar like we did tonight, and then just kick back on the boat and cook something on the pit and people watch for a day or two."

"What else don't I know about you?"

"Hard to say; I'm still discovering who I am. It's late; want to hit the sack or sit on the back of the boat and watch the stars? Speaking of which, ever see so many stars?"

"No, the sky is beautiful. How many stars do you think are up there, a billion?"

"Hard to say, and I bet you and I will never know. What did you decide, Heather? Stay up or go to bed?"

"I am so psyched; let's stay up."

"You got it. It will just take a few minutes to pull the top off, and then we'll have a clear view of the sky off the back. While I take care of the top, why don't you make us something to drink? Also, as long as you're going below, why don't you bring some cheese back with you? It should be in the refrigerator."

"What are you drinking tonight? What can I get the captain of the ship?" asked Heather.

"How about a scotch?"

"One scotch and Colby cheese on the way."

After just a few minutes, Heather emerged from the cabin to find the back deck fully exposed to the outside world. Lucas, noticing how full Heather's hands were, reached for his glass of scotch. Heather placed the cheese, and her glass of wine, on a small table between Lucas and the padded bench on the rear of the deck.

"Lucas, you got something I can cover my shoulders with while we're out here? If so, I'd like to get it before I settle in."

"Look in the closet at the bottom of the steps on the right and you'll find an old shirt I wear when I'm washing the boat. It doesn't look like much, but it's clean."

"Got it!" she yelled from inside the cabin.

This time Heather returned from the lower deck with empty hands, but she had also managed to shed her clothes and replace them with Lucas's shirt. The shirt was an old uniform shirt that nearly reached Heather's knees, with sleeves long enough to almost cover her hands. The shirt could be used for a night shirt, which was exactly what Heather had opted to do.

She headed for the rear bench, and perched directly in front of Lucas. She sat perpendicular to Lucas, with her bare feet on the cushion. She turned and tilted her head to the left to see Lucas. Both of her hands interlocked at her ankles, with her knees under her right cheek. Although the shirt reached her knees when standing, her seated position gave her barely enough fabric to sit on. The front of the shirt gathered in her lap, letting her beautiful, smooth legs rise above.

The deck was dimly lit, with the only light coming in from one of the yellow dock lights in front of the boat. Heather could see a rough outline of Lucas, but his face was in silhouette. To her right, Heather could see boats lining the other side of the cove.

The water was smooth and like a mirror, reflecting the dock lights, the stars, and lights coming from other boats. Since the dock light was located behind Lucas, he was able to see Heather's features. Her eyes were intense and seemed to sparkle. Looking past Heather, Lucas could also see the boats docked on the other side of the two-hundred-foot-wide cove.

"Heather, do you have any idea how pretty, cute, and sexy you look right now? I wish I could capture your look at this moment and remember it forever. I don't have the words to express how beautiful you are."

"You're just saying that because you're horny."

"No, I'm not. Besides, your look isn't about me! It's the truth."

"So you're not horny?"

"I may be, but that still has nothing to do with the way you look."

"If you insist," replied Heather. "Why don't you go get comfortable? I'll guard your drink."

"That sounds like a good idea. I'll be back in thirty seconds." Lucas bolted for the cabin.

In Lucas's absence, Heather took in her surroundings, still in awe. The atmosphere was so peaceful and romantic. *If I could only live like this—feel like this—every day of my life. I wonder where this relationship is going. Maybe this is it: mad, crazy sex. But what about a house, kids, or maybe a boat we both own? Back to reality, Heather. I should appreciate what I have and worry about tomorrow another day.*

"See, that didn't take long," Lucas said upon his return. "You didn't drink my scotch, did you?

"Nope, I said I would guard it. Besides, I never developed a taste."

"Can I pour you another glass of wine? I thought I'd just bring the booze with me to keep us from running back and forth."

"Damn, you pilots are smart! Sorry about that; I'm just playing with you. Please, I'm dry as a bone."

"Heather, how much have you had to drink?"

"I said I was just playing."

"I know, and now I'm playing with you," retorted Lucas. "It's so dark out here I thought I'd leave the cabin door ajar a little; at least then we'll be able to see what we're eating. Speaking of which, where is the cheese?"

"It's on the table. I covered it."

"Thanks. Heather, do you have any idea how attractive you are, the power you possess? Didn't I just ask that question? See, you have me repeating myself."

"Like I told you earlier, I just think you're horny and feeling the effects of the scotch. But you can keep on telling me that if you wish."

Lucas's mood changed from one of conversation to one of reflection and observation. He was mesmerized by the sheer beauty of Heather, still sitting with her knees high, her unbuttoned shirt left her left nipple and her entire hip exposed. Heather's overwhelming beauty seemed to have a hypnotic power over

Lucas. Heather was inviting to Lucas without saying a word. She stared at Lucas as though speaking to his inner being. Lucas couldn't take his eyes off of Heather. He wondered how nature could have created such a perfect body and face. Her legs were fully exposed. Lucas studied them intently, and couldn't help but notice her pubic hair barely extending beyond her obscurely defined thigh. From there, he traced her leg as it led to her innocent baby face, with eyes that would capture the soul of any man. Lucas found himself conflicted. He didn't know whether he should just sit there and enjoy the sight of Heather, lean over and hug her until the sun rose, or make love to her all night. Lucas recognized that feeling conflicted usually led him to do nothing, but he also knew that this wasn't a time for indifference.

Lucas and Heather continued sipping their drinks in total silence, each wondering what the other was thinking. Heather saw this handsome, mysterious fellow, who had changed her life in a matter of months—a fellow who had made her feel alive, loved, and needed. She saw a fellow who had taught her how to appreciate lovemaking and her sexuality. She saw a hunk of a man whom she could wrap her legs around, press against his cock, and grind her hips until he begged for mercy. Heather didn't know whether she should remain seated to enjoy watching Lucas, or if she should allow her hormones to take charge of her actions.

Lucas finally decided to seize the moment. Just watching Heather wasn't enough. He wanted her; he wanted to be inside of her. He was already excited just being so close to this beautiful, sexy woman. Seeing her nearly naked caused his hormones to behave as though they were a part of an experiment that had gone bad. His cock was hard and struggling to escape from his loose shorts.

He rose and moved the table that had been separating them, and then scooted his chair right up to the bench, allowing only enough room for his legs. Leaning toward Heather, he began gently kissing her left ear. Lucas's left arm slipped under and around Heather's legs and his right arm wrapped behind her, allowing his right hand to hold her just below her right breast.

Heather, also in a heightened state of arousal, reacted to Lucas's closeness and his touch. She lifted her head from her knees, turning her face toward Lucas.

Lucas continued exploring her face with his gentle kisses. The softness of his lips, warmth of his breath, and the scent that was uniquely his all moved Heather to a level of excitement that only sex would normally achieve. While caressing Heather with his lips, Lucas dropped his left hand down the underside of her exposed thighs.

As Lucas teased the underside of her legs with a feathery touch, he brushed the pubic hair that provided cover to the warm, wet area between her legs. Although Lucas didn't linger in this area, he did have a brief encounter with her lips, moist even without penetration.

His touch brought Heather close to the edge. She reacted to his touch by turning her body toward Lucas. As she swiveled at the waist, her breasts became almost totally exposed, her nipples erect. She fumbled with the shirt until it dropped wide open, providing Lucas with a clear path to what both had been longing for.

Lucas continued to touch the most sensitive area between her legs. Lucas inserted a finger ever so slightly, and then withdrew it as he toyed with her lips and the softest skin surrounding her sensitive cavern. Her juices were warm and silky smooth.

Heather neared climax, but fought her erotic feelings, hoping to delay her burst into ecstasy. Lucas continued his feathery kisses on her ear and cheek, and then moved to her left breast. He gently took her hard nipple and traced around and around it with his tongue, then gently sucked. Heather arched her back and moaned with pleasure, nearly losing control.

Shifting her focus from her own pleasure to delay an orgasm, Heather slid her hand up Lucas's leg and under his shorts, finally reaching his swollen cock. She began to fondle it, and her own excitement brought her to the most powerful orgasm she had ever felt. Her muscles tightened and her stomach and groin area quivered as waves of pleasure gushed through her body, leaving her in a temporary state of physical exhaustion, unable to move her tightened muscles.

With Lucas's help, Heather removed his shorts. With Lucas still seated, she maneuvered herself on top of his now-exposed and very hard cock, taking direct aim at the wetness between her legs. With her left hand, she took his cock and guided it directly into her. It glided in easily and deep. Heather maneuvered to feel every inch of Lucas as deeply as possible. Lucas was on fire with his mind running wild, *Jeez she feels good, so wet and smooth! My dick feels like it will explode any minute. I wish this feeling would last forever.*

The two were locked in a bear hug, pinned together by Lucas's dick deep in Heather. The instant Lucas filled her cavity,

Heather once again began to quiver as a second orgasm consumed her body. Arching her back and squeezing his dick with her love muscles, she lost control of her ability to do anything but allow her state of euphoria to pass. The only thing Heather could do was to sit there, holding Lucas while her groin pulsated with each wave of erotic energy that passed through her body.

As the impact of her orgasm began to fade, she felt driven to give Lucas the same satisfaction he had given her. She leaned away from Lucas, bracing herself on the bench cushion. She began a rhythmic motion, moving her pelvis in a circular motion, massaging Lucas's dick buried deep inside. Lucas had been excited the moment he sat down, so it didn't take long for him to explode in Heather, with the head of his dick pulsating against the soft, wet walls of Heather's cavern. Lucas's orgasm and his heavy breathing set off another eruption within Heather. She froze with Lucas inside of her as her own orgasm continued to ripple through her body. *Three organisms within 20 minutes, my God, I feel good, but totally used up,* was a thought that continued running happily through Heather's mind. To avoid falling on the deck in complete exhaustion, she leaned forward and lay against Lucas's chest as he also went limp. The two supported one another's weight as they recovered from their trip into ecstasy.

The next day they reversed the process of setting up house on the boat. Since Lucas had to be home by late afternoon for his standby shift, they had to close the boat up and get underway.

On their way home, they relived the night and engaged in idle conversation, starting with what they might have for lunch, going to what each usually had for breakfast. After a couple of minutes of quiet, Heather stopped and looked quizzically at Lucas, wishing that she knew more about him. Heather asked, "Why don't you ever tell me anything about your family life, school, friends, or anything? You know everything about me; my life is an open book."

"And you know everything about me," replied Lucas. "I prefer dark beer over light, red wine over white, you know my GPA, you know what awaits me when I finish school, you know where I go to school, you know what I do at work, you know my favorite foods, you know where I live, you know what my dick looks like! What else is there?" *Why do we keep having this same conversation? I wonder what Heather is looking for.*

"I didn't know you had a boat."

"But you do now. What should I do, carry a notebook around and make a note when I think of something you don't know?"

"Well, you know what I mean. Who are you? You never share your thoughts. I can see when you are happy or sad, but I seldom know what causes either."

"Heather, with me, what you see is what you get—there isn't anything else."

" Ever  since I first saw you, I couldn't get you off my mind, Lucas. I would wake up thinking about you and go to sleep thinking about you. It wasn't just a physical thing with me; you were a person I had to get to know. Even though we have been seeing each other for the past several months, I feel like I still don't know who you are. I feel like you keep me away from your private life."

"Heather, I don't know what to tell you. You seem to want something I can't give you. The person sitting with you right now is the person I am. Can't you just admire a painting without knowing how the artist created it? I understand that you may have questions about my past or other people in my life, but that doesn't change who I am. You think you will have a better understanding of me by hearing about my brother, but you may just end up with even more questions—or even see the real me differently. I have never been one to talk about myself. My experiences, ideas, and beliefs are mine and not for sharing." *What's the big deal? Why can't she understand this?*

"That's just it: you don't share!"

"I do share! I share the thing that most defines me as a person. I share my time, my life...This moment isn't mine, it is ours! That is sharing. When I'm flying and thinking of you, that's sharing! What more could a person ask for than knowing that someone else is allowing them into their personal thoughts throughout the day? That isn't just sharing, it's a giving away of oneself."

"Lucas, I don't think you understand what I am saying."

"And I don't think you understand what I'm saying. Goddamn it, Heather, would you feel better about me if I told you I got drunk and was arrested when I was sixteen?"

"I wouldn't feel better about knowing you were arrested, but I would feel better knowing you were willing to tell me."

"Do you think you would know me better? Incidentally, for the record I've never been arrested."

"No, but—"

Lucas interrupts Heather: "I wear a nine-and-a-half shoe. Know me better now? My waist is thirty to thirty-two inches. Know me better now? I love going down on you. Know me better now? Heather, for us to get along, we have to accept each other for who we *are*, not for who we wish the other person could be or for what we may have been in the past. Maybe it's best these differences come up now—maybe we confused physical attraction with compatibility. Heather, we had a fabulous evening, we do well together, but I think we need to ask ourselves where we're going as a couple."

"Lucas, I don't like this conversation. Let's change the subject."

# CHAPTER TEN
## *Lucas Meets the Feds*

❦

O n Monday, Lucas got up around ten o'clock intending to call the FAA and discuss the citation he and Mike received for flying an airplane without one of the inspections. The first order of business upon waking was to go to the bathroom, as he always did shortly after his feet hit the floor. Following his bathroom routine, he headed straight to the coffeemaker for his first of many morning cups.

With coffee in hand, Lucas went straight to his phone, located near the kitchen table. In light of his Wednesday interview with Global, he felt compelled to hear for himself what was going on with the citation. He placed a notepad and the letter he'd received from the FAA near his phone and then called the individual who'd signed the letter.

After dialing the number contained in the letter, the phone began to ring through. It continued for what seemed a hopeless number of times.

Sure no one would answer, Lucas started to hang up when he heard, "Dean Weaver, hello, hello."

"Oh, uh...Mr. Weaver, this is Lucas Sanders. I received a letter from you about two weeks ago, indicating that I was being cited for flying one of our planes without the hundred-hour inspection."

"This is Lucas Sanders, right?"

"That's correct. I fly for State Side."

"I remember that. What is the case number at the top of the letter?"

"N as in 'November,' four-six-two-nine-zero-three-one."

"OK, Lucas." Weaver paused. "I see you were cited for flying Convair thirty-seven-thirteen-papa without its hundred-hour inspection. You know the FAA takes these regulations seriously, especially when dealing with commercial operators."

"I realize that. I take them seriously as well. After all, it's my neck up there as well as others'. My partner has been looking into this situation. He discovered that the inspection had been completed, but that the entry wasn't made in the logbook."

"Lucas, you realize that if the paperwork is not completed, the inspection never took place."

"I do realize that, but the chief mechanic is responsible for the entry."

"This is true, but you as the pilot in command are responsible for determining that the plane is airworthy. The only way you can do that is to inspect the required paperwork or logbook before you fly the plane. You or Michael didn't do that."

"You're right; we screwed up. But I wasn't the pilot in command."

"I didn't know that. According to our records, you are both qualified as pilot in command on a Convair. It looks like you both got the letter because we didn't know who was acting as the PIC on that flight."

"Well, that was Mike. Can I get a letter from Mike acknowledging that he was PIC on that flight, and get my name off this citation?"

"You do that and your citation will be pulled from your file."

"Otherwise, where is this going? I ask because I have a follow-up interview with Global and can't mess this up."

"The worst-case scenario for a minor violation is that we put a person on a twelve-month probation. As for you and Mike, once the paperwork is received showing that the inspection was completed but the logbook was simply overlooked, this issue can be closed with a note attached to your file for a twelve-month period. We won't charge you with a violation unless something like this happens again. You do understand that a mechanic's mistake can't relieve you from your obligations?"

"I understand that, but just to clarify: you're telling me that if I get that letter from Mike stating that he was the PIC, it will clear me completely?"

"That's correct, but in the meantime, we're waiting for Gold Coast to respond. Until then, this is an open case. We can't do anything until they respond, or you get me the letter from Mike."

"At least I know what I can do to close this out."

"If you want to wrap this up quickly, and it sounds like you do, get that letter from Mike and have Gold Coast send us the information we need."

"I'll work on that today. Now tell me this—when Global does its background check, what will they find?"

"We had an inquiry from them yesterday—hang on just a second; I need to put the phone down to find that file."

A few seconds passed before Weaver returned to the phone.

"Lucas, it looks like they were told there is an active investigation into an FAR violation. No other information was shared."

"That actually sounds worse than it is."

"Don't know what to tell you, Lucas. You may want to take a copy of the letter I sent you and get something from Gold Coast to prove that the investigation is the result of a missing logbook entry and you guys failing to note the missing entry. Get that letter from Mike and take that with you. I'm sorry to say that this kind of violation happens across most commercial operators at one time or another. The most important thing is going to be a letter from Mike stating that he was the PIC. That's going to be your golden ticket."

"Mr. Weaver, I sure appreciate you taking the time to explain all of this to me."

"Glad to be of help. Keep me posted on your trip to Global."

"Sure will. Take care now."

Lucas returned the phone to the cradle and began his morning ritual in preparation for the trip to Gold Coast.

Lucas entered the Gold Coast lobby in the middle of the afternoon during the height of activity. The first person to capture his attention was Heather, who was busy taking care of customers while various corporate pilots made requests and tried to pay bills. Although his mission was to visit with the maintenance group, he couldn't help but take a moment to absorb the sheer beauty of Heather. Her face was like an angel's. Her hair was perfect, with every strand neatly in place. Her miniskirt advertised the beauty of her long, smooth legs. For a brief second, he could feel the warmth of where her legs came together—a feeling others could only imagine.

Returning to reality, his focus shifted to his original mission. With a quick smile and wave to Heather, Lucas proceeded directly to the office belonging to the director of maintenance.

Upon entering the office, Lucas found the person he was looking for behind the desk: Clyde Wilcox, Director of Maintenance for Gold Coast Aviation.

"Good morning, Clyde. I'm Lucas Sanders and I fly for State Side. Mike and I got a letter from the FAA indicating that we violated the FARs by flying the Convair without the hundred-hour inspection."

"Yes, I'm aware of the letter. Mike brought his by the other day. As I recall, Mike went back through all the records and found that the hundred-hour inspection had been completed, but was never entered into the logbook. We can make that correction. It won't be a problem."

"What I need from you, Clyde, is a letter pointing out that you guys made the mistake of not entering the inspection in the logbook, and that the plane's inspection was completed and the plane was airworthy. I have an interview with Global on Wednesday and that incident was reported when they did my background check."

"I can give you a letter, but that citation is for flying the plane without confirming the inspection had been completed. In other words, the FAA is saying you didn't determine the plane was airworthy. Us making the entry or not isn't the issue facing you and Mike. I'm sure the feds want to know why Mike discovered the missing entry long *after* the flight took place. You guys should have called that to our attention the night of the flight. It would have been fixed."

"I know, but Dean Weaver, the inspector, told me to take a letter with me. Will you give me the letter anyway?"

"Of course. Are you flying tonight?"

"That's the plan."

"In that case, I'll leave it at the front desk and you can pick it up later."

"Thanks, Clyde. See you later."

Distraught over his visit with Clyde, Lucas went home without saying anything to Heather. His plan was to get into the swimming pool and reflect on current events, then return to the airport at his usual time.

Arriving at the airport at nine in the evening, Lucas headed straight to Heather to pick up his letter from Clyde Wilcox.

Heather was closing out a fuel bill for another customer, and a strange calmness came over Lucas as he watched her. No longer feeling like he was all alone, he began to relax.

"Good evening, sunshine. You are looking fantastic," he said, sounding upbeat.

"And right back to you," replied Heather. "I saw you earlier, but you never came back. Are you OK?"

"I am. I came by earlier because Dean over at the FAA office suggested that I get a letter from Clyde explaining what happened with the logbook entry. He thought it might be a good idea to take it with me to my interview on Wednesday. Speaking of which, do you have it? He said he would leave it here."

"Sure do. How has your day gone otherwise?"

"Fine. I spent most of the afternoon in the pool worrying about my interview and this stupid citation."

"Look, Lucas: like you would tell me, you can't worry about what has happened. Worrying about the interview isn't going to help either. What you need is a good romp between the sheets."

"As good as that sounds, don't forget I've got to fly tonight, Heather."

"Got ten minutes? I have a storage closet back here. I could use a break from the counter anyway," she said, a playful tone in her voice.

"What happens if someone comes in?"

"They can wait."

"I have a funny feeling this isn't a good idea," said Lucas as he walked toward the end of the counter.

Reaching the end of the counter, Heather held out her hand, took Lucas's wrist, and led him around the corner into a small storage closet with one bare, dim bulb hanging from the ceiling.

Still holding hands, Heather guided Lucas into the closet first, following close behind. Heather's back was to the door and Lucas faced her. With her left hand, Heather began to rub Lucas's cock. With her right hand, she took Lucas's left hand and slid it under her miniskirt and panties, then began to kiss him passionately. Lucas got hard immediately. Heather released Lucas's left hand and began to hug Lucas. Lucas's left hand stayed in place as he began to fondle her.

Lucas had become so hard and large that Heather had difficulty getting his dick released from his pants, and was successful only after undoing his belt and dropping his pants around his knees, followed by his underwear. Heather immediately released her grip on Lucas's underwear, reached under her skirt, and pulled her panties down as Lucas retracted his hand so as not to interfere with her mission. As her panties hit the floor, she steped out of them, leaving a clear path for Lucas.

She took his dick and placed its swollen head at her entrance while Lucas slid his hands under the cheeks of her ass, pulling her slightly off the ground. With a little guidance from Heather, his dick entered her effortlessly and slid in deeply. Both made small adjustments in their positions to get his hard dick in as deeply as possible.

The head of Lucas's dick throbbed as it pressed hard against the inside of Heather's wet cavern. After no more than thirty seconds of penetration, Lucas began to come. His dick throbbed with each wave of ecstasy. Feeling Lucas climax deep inside her was all it took for Heather to let go and do the same, causing her insides to throb around Lucas's dick as her climax repeated itself time and again, draining all of her energy and leaving her limp in Lucas's arms. As Lucas's excitement and energy subsided, so did his ability to hold Heather off the floor. As Lucas lowered Heather, his dick began to slide out, bringing with it a combination of their juices.

"Lucas, do you have any idea how wonderful that was?"

Lucas took a deep breath as he replied, "It was quick but fantastic, and probably the craziest thing we've ever done." *Wow-she is good.*

Heather looked down at her watch and then back at Lucas, "Know how long we've been in here?"

"Tell me."

With a silly grin on her face, she said, "About three minutes."

"That was the best three minutes of my life," said Lucas.

Checking herself and Lucas before leaving the closet, Heather nervously announced, "I have love juice all over my skirt, and it's starting to run down my leg!" She helped tuck the little general in. "You're dripping wet too, Lucas. I think the little general is oozing its cargo. We both need to run to the restroom.

Let's say our good-byes now so we can dash to the restroom and avoid any unnecessary scrutiny, if you know what I mean."

"Sure do. This was crazy, but worth it. Unfortunately, I feel like I peed in my pants."

With that decision behind them, they embraced in the privacy of their closet, each telling the other to have a nice night. Heather immediately scooped her panties from the floor, turned around and opened the door slowly, listening for any unknown customers who might have surfaced. Hearing nothing, she slowly looked around the corner and pushed the door open a little farther. Seeing no one, she immediately stepped out. Certain that they were by themselves, she announced to Lucas that they were clear. He exited quickly and headed straight for the restroom, followed closely by Heather.

Once he'd finished cleaning himself, Lucas left the restroom and headed straight to the flight office, hoping to see Mike.

"Mike," he said upon entering the office. "Glad to see you're here. I have my follow-up interview with Global on Wednesday. They're flying me out early Wednesday and back Wednesday night. I'll need one of the contract pilots to cover me tomorrow night, but I should be back for Wednesday's flight."

"Hang on. Our flight tonight is being assigned to a contract crew and you and I are to take a group over to New York tomorrow in the Lear and come back Wednesday."

"I can't go. Can you find a sub?" Lucas asked, with concern in his voice.

"Don't get excited. There are a ton of pilots out there who would love a little Lear time. I'll make a few calls in a minute. But first, tell me about your interview. Are you OK with the citation from the feds?"

"I'm not really sure. I talked to Dean Weaver from the FAA today and he doesn't think it's a big deal, but suggested that I get a letter from Clyde explaining what happened. He also needs to get a letter from you explaining that you were the PIC that night."

"Hanging me out to dry, are you?"

"You know how the feds are. If a regulation says the pilot in command is responsible for something, they want the PIC held responsible, not the copilot."

"I know; just giving you a hard time. I'll put that letter together for you tonight since we aren't flying. Why don't I leave it at the front desk and you can pick it up whenever you like? Did you get the letter from Clyde?"

"I did, and appreciate your help in this as well."

"Not a problem; that's why they pay us the big bucks."

"Big bucks or not, I appreciate your help. I'm still not sure how Global will see this."

"They should see this like the feds will. You didn't do anything wrong. You haven't violated any regulations. In my book, you're squeaky clean. Lucas, just do your best and be honest and they will do right by you. Besides, I thought they'd already hired you."

"They did, but they wanted to move my start date so I asked if there was anything I could do to keep the original date—the second interview was sort of my idea. That's what triggered another background check. Wish I'd kept my mouth shut."

"You can't worry about that now; I don't see why this would change their decision."

"I hope not. I think I would die. So we're OK for tomorrow and Wednesday?"

"Sure. Take off and relax; enjoy your trip. Don't even worry about Wednesday night. They already pulled both of us from the schedule because of the New York flight."

"Thanks, Mike. I appreciate your understanding and support. If you need me, call. Otherwise, I'll plan on seeing you Thursday evening."

"Go dazzle the big guys!"

While Lucas was still in the area, Autumn arrived uncharacteristically early for her evening shift. Heather immediately interrogated Autumn about her early arrival. Arriving early wasn't her intention, explained Autumn, but she'd had a really bad dinner date. She decided she had two choices, neither of which she liked: she could either stay with her worthless date and make it a long night, or go to work. She chose the latter.

After a few minutes of chitchat, Autumn decided to replenish the popcorn, coffee, and paper for the copier while waiting for her actual shift to begin.

"Heather, they still keep the copy paper in the storeroom back here behind the counter? The last time I looked, there wasn't any there."

"Sure is; I saw some there earlier."

Autumn headed for the supply room, opened the door, and stopped short.

"Heather," she said inquisitively, "I smell the sweet scent of sex in here. Trust me; I know that smell. It almost makes me excited. Come here, and you smell."

Heather walked over to the open door. Careful not to give off any signals that would suggest that she knew anything about what Autumn was talking about, Heather stuck her head out while leaning toward the storeroom, as though trying to get a whiff of what Autumn was talking about without actually going in.

"I don't smell anything, Autumn."

"I may be wrong, but that aroma speaks to me; I love it."

The way the girls were standing, Lucas could only see Heather as he rounded the corner. "Hey Heather," he said. "Great news: we can finish—Oh, hi, Autumn. Didn't see you standing there."

No one said anything. Autumn cocked her head and looked at Heather with an expressionless face, as though saying *Really?*

Heather shrugged and said, "What?"

Lucas looked sheepish and said, "Am I missing something?"

"Lucas, you were saying something to Heather," Autumn said knowingly.

"Oh, uh—I just want to tell her that if anyone looked for me tonight I would be at home. Mike and I were pulled from the flight tonight."

Not satisfied with Lucas's response, Autumn said, "You were telling Heather you could finish something."

"Oh, I don't know. I'm sure it will come to me."

"Lucas, you're right. When the time is right, it will *come* to you, if it hasn't already," retorted Autumn.

"Yes, uh..." Lucas said slowly. "Well, goodnight, ladies. Have a good evening."

Lucas quickly headed for the parking lot.

"OK Heather, what's going on? You and Lucas a couple now?"

"No, we've just gotten to be good friends."

"Bullshit. Is that what it's called when some guy takes you to the lake for the weekend? Good friends? Come clean! This is your buddy Autumn talking."

"It wasn't the weekend; it was one night," responded Heather sharply.

"I see. So one night of fucking means you're just good friends? What would two nights mean?"

"Come on, Autumn. You know I've had a thing for Lucas for a long time."

"I know that, but I always thought he wasn't interested in getting involved. So, Heather, is he a good lay?"

"Autumn, I don't discuss that stuff with others."

"Knock it off, Heather. I'm not 'others.' This is me, Autumn—the person who helped you get fucked the other day."

"Autumn, you don't know that."

"Yes I do. You fucked all weekend." *If he fucked Heather, he'll fuck me again. I'll make that happen.*

"It wasn't all weekend."

"Whatever! How many times did he ring your bell?"

"Autumn, why are you preoccupied with Lucas and me?"

"It's not you and Lucas I'm preoccupied with; it's your sex I want to know about. How long have you been screwing on the job?"

"If you have to know, we had a quickie in the closet. Satisfied?"

"The question is, are you?"

"This is the last comment about Lucas and me. We have good sex and where this is going is anyone's guess. He is a private person and hasn't been looking for a relationship, like you said. We get along well, so time will tell. Period! End of this discussion."

"Well, I still have questions, but I'll wait for a better time."

"There won't be a better time, Autumn," responded Heather in a stern voice.

"Bet I can get more information from Lucas."

"Autumn, leave him alone. I'm going home. You have a good night."

"Easy for you to say; you got fucked tonight and all I had was a stupid-ass date with a moron who couldn't find his dick if you handed it to him. Now I have to think about fuckin' every time I get something from the storeroom."

"Autumn, cut it out and have a good night."

On Wednesday, Lucas caught the first flight to Dallas and headed straight to the Global customer service desk, where he was told to report. Once there, he was told to wait for a rep from HR to swing by and pick him up.

After a twenty-minute wait, a nice young lady named Desiree pulled up on a golf cart with "Global Airlines" painted in large letters across the side. Desiree appeared to be in her early twenties. She had long blond hair and blue eyes and was dressed in a dark suit.

"Hi! My name is Desiree Jackson. Are you Lucas Sanders?

"Sure am."

"Well, climb aboard! Frank Morrison asked me to swing by and pick you up and deliver you to Gil Ferguson, our ops manager. Guess you're going to fly for us?" Desiree asked.

"That's my plan."

"You'll love Global."

"I'm sure I will. I've been looking forward to this since I was a kid."

"Sounds like a dream come true."

"Pretty much," said Lucas.

When they pulled up in front of a door marked "Operations," Desiree said, "We're here. Let me get the door for you." She scooted out of the cart and proceeded to enter a code to unlock the door. With the door open, Desiree stood back to allow Lucas to enter. She told him, "Go on in and tell the receptionist you are here to see Gil. She'll take good care of you."

"Thanks for the ride, Desiree. Have a nice day."

"Good luck—hope to see you around."

"Me, too."

Lucas entered a typical office area—not at all what he'd expected behind a door marked "Operations" at a busy airport. The room was carpeted and had all sorts of pictures hanging on the walls. Some were of the old planes flown when the airline got started, and some were of the new fleet. The atmosphere was warm and pleasant. Lucas proceeded directly to the receptionist, as instructed.

"Hello. I'm Lucas Sanders, here to see Gil Ferguson."

"Yes, we've been waiting for you. Please sign in." The receptionist pointed to a guest book located on the corner of her desk. "Here is a guest badge you need to wear while in this area. Please have a seat and I'll tell Gil you are here."

"Thank you." Lucas located a comfortable-looking chair and took a seat.

Gil emerged from his office and walked straight up to Lucas. Lucas immediately rose and began walking toward Gil, all the while extending a hand.

"Lucas, how you doing today? Your flight OK?

"Sure was. On the wrong side of the cockpit door, but otherwise fine."

"I love it. We'll see what we can do about that. Let's run back to my office to talk for a while, then we'll get you out as quick as we can."

With pleasantries out of the way, Gil and Lucas retreated into Gil's office.

"So, Lucas, we originally had a start date of September first, but it looked like we would have to move you to November. If you recall, that was the purpose of Frank Morrison's call several weeks ago."

"Right. I think that was the worst call I've ever received."

"You'll feel better after today. Following that conversation, we pulled your file. Based on our previous background check, your interview, and experience, we decided to save a seat for you in that September class. We just have one little issue to clear up. Agreeing to bring you back also triggered another background check, and this time we turned up a pending citation from the feds. What can you tell me about that?"

"OK, here is exactly what happened. My partner and I were flying a Convair 440 with a load of freight. We've been flying together for a long time, and although we are both qualified to serve as PIC, Mike has that title and corresponding responsibility—and, I might add, pay. Mike deals with the paperwork component of the flight while I do the preflight and confirm proper loading of the plane. Apparently Mike overlooked the maintenance record one night, because we were both notified several weeks later that we had flown that night without the hundred-hour inspection. In reality, that was not the case. The inspection had been completed, but it had not been entered into the maintenance log we keep in the office. So the maintenance had been done; Mike just missed the fact that it had not been entered into the log. I received that violation letter because we are both qualified as PIC, but the feds didn't actually know who had that responsibility. I brought a letter from the director of maintenance, confirming that the maintenance had been done. And here is a copy of a letter Mike wrote to the feds explaining that he was acting PIC. According to Dean Weaver at the St. Louis FAA office, this letter will clear me completely."

Lucas handed the letters to Gil.

"I see. Lucas, we at Global pride ourselves in hiring the best of the best, and everyone who has interviewed you wants you to be a member of our team. This letter from your partner stating that he was the pilot in command will clear this issue up with us. As a matter of routine, we will do another background check to show that the letter has been removed from your file. We are all looking forward to your arrival in September." Gil gave Lucas a welcoming thumbs-up.

"And I am looking forward to being here," responded Lucas.

"Welcome to Global, Lucas." Gil extended a hand. "Let's go back out into the lobby; we have some additional paperwork for you to complete, because when you return you will be one of us." Gil rose and headed for the door with Lucas in tow.

Approaching the receptionist's desk, Gil said, "Martha, will you begin processing the paperwork for Lucas to start at the academy on September first?" Gil turned to Lucas and extends a hand again. "Welcome aboard. We'll be in touch with details on transportation, housing, and the like. If in the meantime you have any questions, be sure to give me a call. And Martha, will you check the flights to St. Louis and get Lucas out on the first available—and if possible, will you make it first class? Lucas, it has been a pleasure. Have a nice flight home and call me if you need me. Otherwise, we'll see you on September first."

"Thank you so much, Gil. You won't regret this decision."

"I know we won't. Have a nice trip home."

Lucas smiled to himself all the way home. His future was developing as planned. *This is actually happening,* he thought to himself, almost in disbelief.

# CHAPTER ELEVEN
## *Engine Shutdown*

ॐ

By Thursday evening, Lucas hadn't spoken with Heather since his return from Dallas due to other commitments, and was anxious to fill her in on all the details as he knew them. Arriving at the airport as usual, just prior to leaving on a trip to Omaha, Lucas told Heather that when he got back he would have to make a quick trip to his apartment, get cleaned up, and go to school.

Knowing Lucas wouldn't be by that night, Heather set an alarm to go off thirty minutes before Lucas's ETA. Her plan was to listen for Mike and Lucas to call the tower once they got near St. Louis. She wouldn't see Lucas or talk with him, but hearing him would be comforting. Her portable radio was already set to the approach control and tower frequencies. When her alarm went off, she wouldn't even need to get out of bed. Instead, she would be able to roll over and turn her radio on, and wait to hear that comforting voice.

In the meantime, Mike and Lucas headed back to St. Louis. During their down time, they found opportunities to reminisce about their memorable experiences, recognizing that their time together was now limited. As they flew, each shared favorite memories, at times erupting in uncontrollable laughter.

"Mike, look at the glow to the east. It won't be long before we'll need our sunglasses."

"Sure enough. I hate these late-night flights. Even if the flight itself is short, when you return with the sun coming up, it feels like you've been flying all night. You got school today?"

"Sure do. Got an important final in one of my psychology classes."

"How are you going to take a test after flying all night?"

"Good question. My plan is to go home, shower, and drink lots of coffee. Actually, I hope the shower tricks my body into thinking I just got out of bed."

"Some trick! If it works, let me know. Feel that vibration?"

"A little. Let me turn the auto sync off and see what that does."

"Still there," Mike confirmed. "I think it's coming from the left engine."

"I don't know, Mike; you can see the engines are in sync. You think it's the left side?"

"I can't tell for sure, but I think so."

"Mike, I'm going to slowly adjust the RPM on the left engine—let's see if the vibration changes."

"Stop! That's making it worse!"

"Yeah, now I can feel it in the controls. This isn't good," said Lucas.

"Lucas, you focus on flying the plane and I'm going to go through the engine shutdown procedure on the left side. The plane is yours."

"Got it."

"OK. Here I go; ignore all the red lights for a second."

Over the next twenty or thirty seconds, Mike went through the engine shutdown checklist, which included shutting down and isolating various systems.

"The left side is feathered and now it's isolated. Lucas, you doing OK with one engine?"

"I am. It sure got quieter, but at least that vibration went away."

"Yeah, I think we were about to throw a blade from the prop. That wouldn't have had a happy ending. When you go to school this morning, I want you to be thankful that you aren't the subject of someone's news report."

"I hear ya. It sure is smoother, isn't it, and slower? This is going to change our ETA." Lucas began the process of amending their arrival time. "I'll let Center know what's going on.

Lucas: "Kansas City Center, this is Convair thirty-seven-thirteen-papa."

Controller: "Convair three-seven-one-three-papa, Kansas City Center."

Lucas: "One-three-papa. Just want you to be aware that we have an engine shutdown and will be slowing down, but otherwise everything is OK. Will you tack on about twenty minutes to our ETA? Once we get things stabilized, I'll give you a new speed."

Controller: "Understood, one-three-papa. Do you need priority handling?"

Lucas: "Just let St. Louis Approach know that we prefer a straight in, and we don't want any go-arounds?"

Controller: "Roger, one-three-papa. Will notify St. Louis Approach, and don't worry about reporting your speed; I can see it coming down on the radar."

Lucas: "Kansas City, one-three-papa, it looks like you need to clear the airspace below. I don't think I can maintain this altitude."

Controller: "Roger, one-three-papa. I'll clear the airspace for you, and in just a few miles I'm going to turn you over to St. Louis approach."

Lucas: "One-three-papa."

"Lucas," Mike asked, "you doing OK or do you need some help?"

"I'm fine for now."

Controller: "Convair three-seven-one-three-papa, contact St. Louis Approach on one-two-six-point-seven—have a safe arrival."

Lucas: "Roger, one-three-papa, we'll be fine. Mike, why don't you take over the radio so I can focus on flying the plane?"

"You got it."

Mike: "St. Louis Approach, this is Convair three-seven-one-three-papa checking in with information delta, and we have our left engine shut down."

Not completely awake, Heather heard Mike's voice calling approach control, but wasn't sure what he'd said about an engine.

Controller: "This is St. Louis Approach Control, one-three-papa, understand you have an engine shut down. Are you declaring an emergency?"

Mike: "Negative, but we can't do any go-arounds and we would like a straight in on one-two-right."

Controller: "One-three-papa, maintain your present heading and expect to intercept the final approach course in about twelve miles. How many souls on board?"

Mike: "One-three-papa, there are two of us on board. Lucas, ya ever wonder when we became souls and not people?"

"Rather impersonal, isn't it?"

"Still OK at the controls? You want to complete the landing?" asked Mike.

"Sure, I'm doing fine; I'll take it all the way in, but once we get it slowed down, you'll have to take the steering."

"Right," responded Mike.

Controller: "One-three-papa, the tower has been advised of your situation and other traffic is being held. You should also expect equipment on the north taxi strip, awaiting your arrival."

Mike: "One-three-papa."

Heather was now fully aware of what was going on. "Equipment" was another word for fire trucks and other emergency vehicles. Panic took a grip on Heather. She'd flown enough to know that, based on his last position, Lucas would touch down in about fifteen minutes. If she left the apartment now, she would probably get there just in time for touchdown. Grabbing whatever she could find to put on, she dashed out the door with car keys in one hand and the radio in the other.

"I'll tell you this, Mike," Lucas said, "at least it's daylight. That should make this process a little easier."

"I agree. Still doing OK?"

"I'm fine."

Controller: "Convair three-seven-one-three-papa, contact the tower on one-one-eight-point-five."

Mike: "Roger, one-three-papa."

Mike: "Tower, this is Convair three-seven-one-three-papa with you."

Controller: "Convair one-three-papa, you're number one cleared to land on one-two right."

Mike: "Roger, one-three-papa. And one-three-papa won't have the reversers—we're going to need to let roll out, so clearing the runway may take a little time."

Controller: "Not a problem, one-three-papa. Take your time."

As Heather rushed to get to the airport, Lucas lined up the Convair with the runway. *Ok, I can't fuck this landing up. I have too much to do today to deal with a bent airplane,* Lucas thought to himself.

Mike and Lucas landed without incident and limped to Gold Coast Aviation, where the Convair would spend the day getting a thorough checkup.

As Lucas exited the plane, Heather rushed to him and leaped into his arms, wrapping her legs around his waist and her arms in a bear hug around his neck.

"Hey, Heather! What's up? Why are you here?" He gently lowered her to the ground.

"I was listening to my monitor. I heard what was going on and couldn't just sit there wondering how you were doing. I couldn't stand the suspense, so I threw on whatever was lying around, and here I am."

"Well, everything is fine; we just had a little issue with one of the engines."

"I was so worried."

"You shouldn't worry about this stuff. It worked out fine. Besides, coming here wouldn't help the situation."

"I know, but I couldn't just sit at home! Are you going home or to school?"

"I need to make a quick stop at home and then go to school, otherwise I'd love to have breakfast with you. Why don't you go home and go back to bed, and I'll swing by after school?"

"If I have to. I just don't want to let go."

"I'm OK and you will be too."

"If you insist."

# CHAPTER TWELVE

## *Visibility Near Zero*

⚜

A s usual, Lucas arrived at the airport around nine o'clock in the evening for an estimated ten thirty departure. Departure times were always an estimate, because no one ever knew exactly when the cargo would arrive at the airport, much less be loaded. On the way to the airport, it was obvious that things would be a little different, at least during departure. The fog was so thick, he could hardly see to drive and had to creep along at a blazing speed of twenty miles per hour.

Once at the airport, everything was pretty much normal except that the cargo was late because of the fog. The same fog slowed down other flights and kept the lobby quiet. Mike had not yet arrived, but that wasn't a big deal since the departure time had been pushed back. With nothing else to do, Lucas went ahead and performed the preflight, and completed all of the paper-work that could be completed without having the cargo weight and other documentation.

Still without Mike or cargo, Lucas felt that the best way to pass the time would be to grab a cup of coffee and check in with Heather.

"Hey, Heather," he said, "where did all your customers go? Scare them away?"

"This place has been dead all night. Mr. Lucas, I wouldn't guess you'd want to try the closet again?"

"I'm not so sure that was a good idea. How did things go with Autumn after I left? In fact, I'd almost forgotten about that."

"How could you forget about the closet?"

"It wasn't the closet I almost forgot about; it was our encounter with Autumn."

"Oh, so want to step into my closet? Autumn won't be in until late; she already called."

"I'm still not so sure that is a good idea."

"Come here, big boy." Heather used her index finger to bring him closer, and walked to the end of the counter.

"Heather, what are you up to? Have you always been this horny?"

"Why do you ask? Besides, you're the one who makes me horny. Come over here! Let's see what we can get *you* up to."

"I don't know that we should be fooling around, Heather."

"Come on, no one is here. What would it hurt?"

"The problem is we're expecting people. Besides, you never answered my question."

"What was the question?"

"How did you and Autumn make out when we had that little encounter?"

"Autumn and I didn't make out; that was you and me. And it wasn't a little encounter. As I recall, it was distinctly large."

"Heather, will you knock it off? You know what I mean. You sure seem to be in a playful mood tonight."

"That's because I can't get enough of the little general."

"Well, I see more of the little general in your future. Now tell me about Autumn."

"She asked a lot of questions, and I answered a few. I think she has a thing for you. The way she asked questions suggested there was more there than just curiosity. Anyway, the conversation just died and I left. Now are you going to come over here or not?"

Lucas was standing at the edge of the counter, directly in front of Heather.

"Now you're mine," said Heather.

As soon as she said those words, Mike pulled in right behind the cargo truck.

"Sorry, Heather," Lucas said. "Next time."

As Mike walked through the door, Lucas announced that everything was ready to go, except for a few entries on the flight manifest. Not wanting to delay the flight any longer, they both proceeded to the plane. Mike went straight to the cockpit and got their clearance. Lucas normally took care of that, but he wanted to make sure the cargo was properly loaded and secured. Convinced that everything in back was secured, Lucas proceeded to the cockpit. Once there, he found that Mike was waiting for him and had everything ready to go. Lucas buckled in, grabbed the checklist from the sunshield, and began his routine

"Mike, do you have the Alton approach plate for our emergency alternate? If not I'll get mine out."

"No need; I have it. The visibility there is running around a half mile. At least we can get in there is we do have an emergency. I wouldn't even want to try to get back in here."

"Mike, I don't mind telling you I don't like this shit!"

"No kidding—getting out will be our biggest problem, though. This fog is only a few hundred feet thick. Lucas, you ready to start on the right?"

"Sure, let's do it. I'll start the count. One, two, three..."

Counting blades was a duty foreign to the non-pilot population, and reminded Lucas of how unique his flying duties were. No one would ever guess that, when firing up the engines, each time a blade reached the top position it was counted to ensure there wasn't a hydraulic lock in any cylinder. After twelve blades, the captain would turn the ignition switch on for that engine, which would usually fire right up, letting smoke bellow out from the exhaust stacks. The same procedure was then followed for the other engine.

"OK, Lucas," Mike said, "you got the radio—let's go."

Lucas: "Ground Control, this is Convair three-seven-one-three-papa at Gold Coast. Ready taxi with information foxtrot."

Controller: "Convair three-seven-one-three-papa, taxi to runway one-two right. Information gulf is current. The only change is in visibility, which continues to change—the last RVR was 1,000 feet. I'll keep you posted as you taxi."

Lucas: "Thanks, one-three-papa. Is this Jack?"

Controller: "No, this is Paul. Jack worked an earlier shift today."

Lucas: "Are you working both ground and the tower tonight?"

Controller: "Just ground for now.

I don't think we've spoken before," Lucas said. "You don't sound familiar. Are you new to St. Louis?"

Controller: "I came down from Springfield last week. This is my first evening shift."

With a smile, Lucas responded, "Welcome to sunny St. Louis."

Controller: "Thanks, but Springfield wasn't any better."

"Any reports from other departures?" Lucas asked.

"No, you guys are the only ones I've worked in the last hour. This fog has most everything shut down. Global got a clearance a little while ago, but haven't heard from him since."

Global Pilot: "Global six-fifty-two is still here. We'll be ready for a push back shortly."

Controller: "Roger, six-fifty-two—give me a call when ready."

"Mike, I can't see shit!" Lucas said. "Stop! Hang on while I get my window open—I'm going to have to stick my head out the window to see the edge of the taxi strip."

Lucas proceeded to crank the side window open. It was a struggle to see the ground around the main gear. The side window frame was just below his shoulder, and with his belt fastened, Lucas was lucky to get most of his head through the window. It didn't take long to feel the effects of a damp evening and a giant propeller turning near his head. Lucas suddenly longed for the peace and security of being inside.

Lucas momentarily pulled his head back in and looked at Mike, saying, "All right, we can go again, but stay left. Can you see the intersection, Mike?"

"Shit! I can't even see the fuckin' centerline much less the intersection."

"I don't see where you've got a choice, Mike. You're going to have to stick your head out the window, too."

Frustrated, Mike mumbled to himself, "I don't believe this shit. Glad no one can see us."

Lucas felt compelled to tell the Global pilot about their experience. "Global six-five-two? Is that right? You still on?"

"Sure are, what ya got?"

"This is Convair one-three-papa. We can't see squat to taxi—just thought you would want to know."

"Thanks. Not sure what we're doing yet. We're already an hour late for departure."

"We are, too."

"Mike, you see any better yet?" asked Lucas.

"Fuck no."

"Mike, it's going to take forever to get to the other end of the runway."

"I know."

Global Pilot: "Ground Control, this is Global six-fifty-two, gate thirty-two, ready to taxi with information gulf."

Controller: "Global six-fifty-two, taxi to runway one-two right; give way to a Convair passing right to left."

Global Pilot: "Global six-fifty-two, yield to the Convair."

"Mike, I don't like the sound of that," Lucas said in an anxious voice. "Ground, this is Convair one-three-papa. We can't see anything out here. Except for being on taxiway alpha, we don't even know where we are—don't let Global get together with us out here."

Controller: "Roger, one three papa."

Controller: "Global six-fifty-two, hold your position. I will tell you when you can proceed."

Global Pilot: "Roger. Six-fifty-two, holding our current position."

Controller: "Convair one-three-papa, Global is going to hold for you. Let me know when you reach the departure end of one-two right."

Lucas: "Will do, one-three-papa."

Controller: "Global six-fifty-two, what is your current position?"

Global Pilot: "Don't know; we have the same problem as the Convair. I know we haven't reached taxiway alpha yet."

Controller: "OK, stay put. I'll let you know when you can proceed."

Global Pilot: "Six-fifty-two."

"Lucas, where do you think we are?" Mike asked.

"Fuck. I don't know, on a taxi strip?"

"I understand that. Think we will be able to see the end of the taxiway?"

"Mike, I don't have a clue, but we don't have an option but to continue. I've never heard of anyone just shutting down on a taxi strip, but I guess we could."

"I guess, but what do we do then? We don't even know where we are."

"I suppose they could send a car out to find us. Mike, you ever see anything like this?"

"No, but hallelujah, I think we've reached the end!"

"Mike, I've got to tell you: I'm exhausted just taxiing to the runway."

"Yeah, this is a terrible way to start a trip," responded Mike.

At about the same time Mike declared them ready for departure, Global checked in over the outer marker on a final approach to land on the same runway Mike and Lucas intended to use.

"Lucas," said Mike, "this should be interesting!"

"I'd like to see how he pulls this off. Tower, this is Convair one-three-papa. Captain says he has his courage up, so I guess we're ready to go on one-two right."

"Convair one-three-papa, hold short: landing traffic."

"Hold short, one-three-papa," replied Lucas. "Mike, he should be here in about a minute—want to place any bets on the outcome?"

"I don't think so; I know how this approach will end."

"Global three-twenty-nine executing a missed approach."

As Global announced their missed approach, Mike and Lucas could barely see the bottom of the plane as it passed over the threshold of the runway. They could hear the engines spooling up to climb power.

"What do you think, Mike? Odds are the crew never saw any part of the runway."

"Now *that* I would bet on," murmured Mike.

Controller: "Roger Global three-twenty-nine. I show Indianapolis as your alternate, maintain your present heading and contact departure one-one-nine point-nine. Global three-twenty-nine—good day."

Controller: "Convair one-three-papa: turn left three-six-zero, cleared for takeoff on runway one-two right."

"One-three-papa," Lucas said. "OK, Mike. I'll call the numbers as usual, but I think we both need to watch for the centerline."

"I'll buy that. Let me get the landing lights on and see if that helps." The lights turned on. "Wow, that's too much glare, but I don't see a choice. You?"

"No, let's let her rip."

With his right hand, Mike moved the throttles forward to takeoff power while Lucas followed the throttles with his left hand. As the power came up on both engines, the instruments seemed to move in unison. Everything came to life. Various warning lights went out while other lights came on, indicating that systems were functioning properly. The airplane began to accelerate quickly.

"OK, Mike, everything's in the green and there's forty-five knots."

"Coming up on V1."

Right after Lucas announced that V1 had been reached, a loud noise grabbed his attention. It was a noise that sounded like an engine backfiring.

"Mike we're losing an engine," announced Lucas.

The Convair continued to accelerate.

"MIKE, GODDAMN IT, WE'RE LOSING AN ENGINE," yelled Lucas as he turned his attention away from the runway to look at Mike.

Mike responded by pulling the throttles of both engines and saying, "Lucas, pull the flaps—T handle."

Mike applied heavy breaking and put both engines in full reverse. While Mike tried to bring their beast to a halt, Lucas held the wheel to prevent control damage from the changing air patterns. Lucas called the tower.

"Tower, one-three-papa is aborting!"

Controller: "One-three-papa, need the equipment?"

Lucas: "Negative—stand by, tower."

"Lucas," Mike said, "got any idea where we are? You see any markers?"

"None! We should have used about four thousand feet, so there should be lots of runway in front of us."

Lucas: "Tower, one-three-papa."

Controller: "One-three-papa, go ahead."

Lucas: "One-three-papa: we were losing an engine and had to shut things down. We got her stopped, but we're lost on the runway. If you can hold the traffic, we're going to stay on the centerline and follow it to the end."

Controller: "That's approved, one-three-papa—give me a call when you clear the runway."

One week later, Lucas could still vividly recall their slow, deliberate return to Gold Coast, still full of the precious cargo. That trip was to be Lucas's last trip with State Side and he was disappointed that it ended as it did. He never found out what was wrong with the engine.

Lucas planned to take a little time off for graduation, and a little more to vacation before reporting to Global for his new job.

# CHAPTER THIRTEEN

## *Ready For Departure*

❧

The ceremony for summer graduates wasn't as lavish as the one held in May for the regular graduating class, but it still had the requisite boring speakers. Lucas tuned the speakers out by thinking not only about his past, but about what his life looked like in the moment. He questioned the wisdom of spending his time reliving the past. Reflecting briefly on the past never hurt anyone, but to dwell on it made no sense to him.

*It's my future I should be thinking about,* he said to himself. *When I think of my future, I see a nearly blank canvas. I only have to decide what I want my future to look like. Therein lies the problem. I am smart enough to know that I have the ability to do whatever I want, and that my future will be the result of my actions. I won't be able to blame anyone else if I screw things up.*

*I am graduating with my degree in psychology. I have a fantastic job that pays well and have an even better one waiting for me in a few weeks. I have a beautiful Corvette, fantastic boat, nice apartment: life is good. I don't think I need to worry about my immediate future. Seems like my career is off to a good start.*

*As for my personal life, Heather has become an important part of it, but she is always preoccupied with my past, or who I am, or something like that. We have fantastic sex. She is beautiful, kind, and loving. I think she would do anything for me. But how can I give serious consideration to making a future with someone who won't accept me for the person I am today? This business of wanting to know more about me is a puzzle; guess I'll never understand it.*

*Then there's my new job waiting for me. I start my training with Global in about four weeks. I will have a crazy schedule for at least six months, perhaps even a year or longer. I have always focused on one thing at a time. Lately it's been school, then my job, and then Heather. I won't have school to deal with, but the Global training and transition to another plane will require a lot of bookwork and time. At this point, I'm not sure I will have the time to give Heather the attention she wants, much less deserves. Is it right for me to ask Heather to sit tight and just wait for me to get my life organized? She could be dating other people. Who knows, she could fall madly in love with next person she meets. Besides, I still can't stop thinking about Morgan. It pains me to think of having a serious relationship with another woman. Dating and sex is one thing, but Heather is looking for a long-term commitment and I can't do that. The way I felt when I lost Morgan was almost more than I could stand. I just can't take that chance again. I owe it to Heather to be completely honest about my feelings. I just don't see her understanding that my doubts are a result of thinking about what is best for her.*

*I'm not going to say anything to Heather today—I need to get this graduation behind me—but tomorrow is a different story. The first order of business is to be completely honest with Heather. The truth has always served me well, and I see no need to change that approach now.*

*I will put my plan into motion tomorrow, but first I need to reflect on this to make sure I'm doing the right thing.*

Immediately following the ceremony, Lucas found Mike and Heather mingling with the crowd of proud onlookers.

"Hey! Mike, Heather, the two of you apparently made it to the end."

"Lucas, that was a nice graduation and you should feel proud of your accomplishment!" Heather gave Lucas a big hug and a kiss. "I know how much you put into your education while working a demanding, full-time job. Way to go!"

"Heather's right," said Mike. "You've worked hard for this, and I am so proud of you. Most people I know would've quit some time ago." Turning toward Heather, Mike asked, "What are you two going to do to celebrate?"

"Don't have any concrete plans," Lucas said. "What would you like to do, Heather?"

"This is your day; you decide. Whatever you choose is fine by me."

"For the first time in a long time, I don't have any homework and I'm not on standby at the airport, so why don't we go to that restaurant on top of the hotel downtown—the one that rotates? Can't think of the name off hand, but we could have a nice meal and then go for a moonlit swim at my place."

"I think that sounds like a wonderful way to celebrate," responded Heather.

Mike extended a hand to Lucas for one last congratulatory comment, and then looking at Heather said, "You lovebirds have a nice evening, and don't stay out too late!" He gave Heather a wink as he turned to walk away.

"Heather, I can't believe this chapter in my life is finished. I feel a little at odds. I don't have anything with which to occupy my thoughts."

"Mr. Lucas," she said in a playful voice, "I'll give you something to occupy your thoughts tonight, and in the meantime, you just think about it."

"Heather, you really tickle me. I'm glad we got together. But now we have a decision to make: do we go straight to dinner, or do I run you home now and pick you up later?"

"Can we go later? I would like to freshen up."

"I'll run you home, then we can both freshen up and I'll pick you up at seven. Sound like a plan?"

"Sounds good to me."

Heather, once home, was determined to make the evening special for both Lucas and herself. A quick shower seemed to be in order, followed by shaving her legs while sitting on the edge of the tub. Legs smooth as silk, her attention turned to her bikini area for a quick trim. All twenty nails received a touch-up with pearl-colored polish that complemented her outfit. Applying just the right amount of makeup—essential to make her complexion flawless—completed the process of putting her body in shape for the evening. The last step before donning her favorite miniskirt—a black silk skirt with a matching strapless top—was to select a pair of panties that would make her feel both elegant and just a little naughty. A black thong did the job. Sandals with rhinestones showed off her freshly painted toenails and completed her outfit.

As Heather slipped into her sandals, she heard her doorbell ring. Heather made her way to the front door. Opening the door, she found Lucas standing there like a date picking up his girl for the prom. He wore black shoes, gray slacks, and a blue blazer with a white shirt.

"Heather," he said, "you're elegant tonight! You're beautiful, but of course you always are."

"Well, thank you. Give me just a minute to throw a few things together and I'll be ready."

Heather retreated to the bedroom to get fresh underwear, a bikini, a toothbrush, and a pair of shorts and a blouse. She tossed her essentials into a small overnight case and returned to Lucas, who still stood near the door of her apartment.

"I'm ready if you are," announced Heather as she approached her waiting date.

"Let's do it."

Lucas stepped out of the apartment and turned to face Heather as she stepped out and then turned back toward the closed door to lock it. Door secured, Lucas took Heather's hand and led her to the right side of the car, where he opened the door and assisted Heather into the car.

*Getting into a Corvette in a miniskirt isn't any more difficult than if I were wearing shorts,* Heather thought, *but it can't be done ladylike.*

*I think I just gave Lucas a preview of dessert. Who cares? Hope he enjoyed it.*

Belted in, Lucas and Heather motored their way to the city, where Lucas had made reservations for an eight o'clock dinner. Their restaurant was located on top of a hotel overlooking the city, including the Gateway Arch. The restaurant rotated, so it didn't matter where they started their dinner, since they eventually saw the entire view. Both Lucas and Heather were in a festive mood.

"Heather, it doesn't matter what you want for dinner or to drink," Lucas said. "This is our night. You want it, we'll get it."

Lucas and Heather celebrated until the restaurant closed. There was no shortage of food or drink—especially drink. As Lucas and Heather began to exit the restaurant, it became apparent that Lucas was in no condition to drive. Being a responsible person, Lucas hailed a cab. In no time, the cab dropped Lucas and Heather off at Lucas's apartment. Although not stumbling drunk, neither felt any pain and both remained in their party mood. It was nearing midnight, but the party went on.

"Heather, let me get a bottle of wine and let's go swimming."

"I would love to, but it looks like the pool is closed."

"Nope, they just turn the lights out at eleven, I assume to discourage late-night partying."

"Like we're about to do."

"Not exactly like we're about to do. I think what they're trying to discourage is more than a party of two. I don't expect we'll make much noise. In fact, I would just as soon not call any attention to our presence."

"You're forgetting one thing."

"What's that, Heather?"

"My swimsuit is in your car."

"You'll be OK. Let me go get that wine."

"If you say so," Heather said.

While waiting for Lucas to return, Heather stood there, surveying the area. Much as she had suspected, the complex was dead, with no signs of life anywhere. Even with the sounds of crickets, there was an eerie quiet on that dark, moonless night.

As Lucas emerged from the apartment, Heather could see that he had retrieved two bottles of wine instead of one, as well as two plastic wineglasses. A grocery bag hung from his right arm, and he'd draped a blanket over his head so that it almost covered his eyes.

Seeing that Lucas had his hands full, Heather darted to his aid and took away one bottle and the blanket. Not only was Lucas relieved to have help, he no longer looked so silly. Between the alcohol and the moonless sky, the two found it difficult to walk in a straight line, and the two supported each other as they made their way to the pool. Heather and Lucas were the only ones out, so the entire pool was theirs for the taking. It was late, dark, and quiet. Once there, the two dropped the blanket within a step or two of the water and, after being comfortably seated, spread their goodies out within arm's reach. Heather checked the grocery bag and found that Lucas had brought cheese to go with their wine.

Lucas leaned on his right arm with his legs spread out within inches of Heather. Heather sat facing Lucas, with her legs crossed in front of her. Such a position required Heather's skirt to be hiked to her waist, but it was dark and no one was around so she let it. With bottles tapped and wineglasses full, Lucas proposed a toast to the future.

They touched glasses and each said, "To the future."

"What do you say, Heather: up for a little swim?"

"I would love to take a dip in the pool, but my suit is back at the hotel in your car."

"Look around: there isn't anyone here, and this is a dark night. I plan to go skinny-dipping. You can too."

"That would be cool. Do you really think we can?"

"Watch me."

Standing, Lucas released his belt, unzipped his pants, and pulled his slacks and underwear off in one motion. His socks were next, followed by his shirt. Sitting there naked, he raised his glass and said, "Your turn." Then he took a sip of wine.

With Lucas's encouragement, Heather pulled her blouse over her head and tossed it on the growing pile of clothes. Her bra followed her blouse. Heather leaned back to pull off her skirt and panties, then added them to the pile.

Sitting there naked, Heather raised her glass and said, "Here's to us." She also took a sip of wine.

Both were naked, both sipped their wine, and neither said anything. Heather was about three feet in front of Lucas. Her legs were crossed, with her knees nearly touching the pool deck. Lucas could only see her major features. Her breasts were distinguishable, but the rest of her body was cloaked in darkness.

Lucas's feet were flat on the pool deck, with his knees together just under his chin. His features were also ill-defined, with only his dick protruding between his legs and pointing upward in an otherwise darkened atmosphere.

"Heather, how about that swim?"

"Let's go," responded Heather.

Lucas was first to his feet, so he reached down to assist Heather. The edge of the pool was only a few feet away, so the walk was short. Heather was the first one in the pool, followed by Lucas.

"Heather, I love to go skinny-dipping. I feel liberated with my business just hanging free and unencumbered."

"I know what you mean; I think this is bringing the devil out in me. Incidentally, the last time I noticed, which was just before you got into the water, your dick wasn't exactly hanging."

"For what it's worth, the little general has a mind of his own. Out of respect for you, he's just standing at attention."

"I bet he is. Seems like that's the way he stays. You skinny-dip before, Lucas?"

"I have, but never with someone else in the pool. I think I prefer it this way."

"Lucas, you bring the little general within arm's reach and I'm going to kidnap him!" Lucas and Heather just moved around in the shallow end for a while, with Lucas occasionally taking a lap for the exercise. Between occasional bursts of energy, both found themselves back at the edge closest to their wine. Their random swimming continued until Heather spotted a flotation device someone had left behind.

With the floatie tucked under her arms, Heather propelled herself to the deep end, where she just allowed her arms and legs to hang. She found the water, the wine, and having Lucas nearby, to be totally relaxing. Almost completely submerged, she could spread her legs wide apart, feel the freedom of being nude, and still no one was the wiser.

Again and again, Lucas and Heather gravitated back to their waiting wineglasses. At one point, Lucas leaned against the side of the pool, wineglass in hand, when Heather arrived with the same intention. With Heather's wineglass now directly behind Lucas, the shortest distance between her glass and her current position brought her directly in front of Lucas.

Being the playful person Lucas was, he decided not to move or hand the wine to Heather, but instead to have her work for her reward. Heather could see that retrieving her glass of wine would require a solo effort. Paddling directly in front of Lucas while still cradling her floatie, she tried to reach over Lucas by placing her right hand on his shoulder and pulling herself higher, putting her within reach of her glass. Lucas found himself staring directly at her left breast. The temptation was too much for him. With his wine in his right hand, he stretched his arm out to avoid a spill, wrapped his left arm around Heather's bottom, and pulled her close. At the same time, he leaned forward and placed Heather's left breast in his mouth. Her nipple was hard.

Although Heather hadn't lost sight of her original mission—to get her wine glass—Lucas was definitely changing her focus. Wine glass is in hand, she preferred to simply hold the glass while Lucas sucked on her left nipple. Lucas's stimulation caused Heather's senses to come alive, heightening her awareness that the two were naked and alone in the pool.

Heather began to release her stretch, put her glass on the pool deck, and move both hands to the top of Lucas's shoulders. Lucas, sensing Heather's interest in returning to the water, allowed her to settle back into the water.

She began to recede back into the pool, sliding down Lucas's chest and stomach until the folds between her legs met his dick, at which point she hesitated, feeling an opportunity to tease Lucas. Half submerged, and with hands still on Lucas's shoulders, Heather lifted herself very slowly and then relaxed, allowing Lucas's dick to barely enter her well-lubricated cavern. Heather's own juices, plus the pool water, enabled Lucas to slide in effortlessly.

Lucas, aware of Heather's intention, set down his glass and held her waist with both hands. Heather continued to play with Lucas's emotions through his dick. Being somewhat buoyant from the water, her movements were effortless. Lucas could feel the head of his dick throb and his nuts tighten every time he entered Heather. Reaching his limit of being teased, Lucas, with his hands on Heather's hips, pulled her downward while thrusting his dick deeply into her. As Heather felt her insides fill with his dick, she took a deep breath and threw her head back while tossing her floatie to the side.

Lucas scooted his feet forward, allowing himself to lean more steadily against the wall of the pool and provide more room for Heather's legs. His shift in position allowed Heather to wrap her legs around Lucas and cross her feet behind him. Holding Lucas with her legs enabled Heather to lean back, with a portion of her weight resting directly on Lucas's hips. They were pinned together, with his dick now buried deep inside of her.

Heather moved her hips in a circular motion to feel every bit of Lucas she could. Lucas's dick was totally inside Heather, with his nuts pressing against her ass. Feeling her insides filled with Lucas almost caused Heather to lose control. Heather was buoyant, so holding her in this position was not a challenge for Lucas. Both breathed hard, and neither was content to simply have Lucas's dick deep in Heather. Both were restless, wanting to make the other come. Each began to move while stimulating the other. Lucas rotated Heather's hips, causing his dick to stimulate every inch of Heather's most sensitive area. Heather moved her whole body, causing the head of Lucas's dick to be massaged from within her.

Finally, Heather came, unable to take the stimulation any longer. Heather's legs tightened around Lucas and her muscles tightened around his dick. With Heather immobilized, Lucas continued to play with her with his dick. Without warning, Heather came a second time, but this time her grip was so intense, his dick became frozen inside of Heather. Heather's legs were still tight around Lucas. Her hands held his shoulders as she leaned back, breathing hard.

Once Heather regained control of her body, she began moving up and down with determination, nearly allowing Lucas's dick to come out before driving it deep inside. In addition to her stroking movements, she squeezed his dick, and in no time Lucas came. The head of his dick had become so sensitive, he gripped Heather's waist and held her tight while his dick felt like it was exploding with each impulse of emotional energy. Wave after wave, Lucas could feel a euphoric eruption from his balls, through his dick, and to the rest of his body. Even his balls felt like they were bursting as they released their cargo deep inside Heather.

Totally exhausted, they held each other close as their bodies returned to some state of normalcy. Finally, after some fifteen minutes of just holding each other, Lucas and Heather began separating. Lucas lifted Heather just enough for his dick to withdraw, and then lowered her so she could stand on the bottom of the pool.

Heather began to walk up the steps to exit the pool. Heather put her right foot on the pool deck, and Lucas reached between her legs, cupping her privates with his right hand. Heather froze when she felt Lucas's hand between her legs, beginning to explore her soft area. With one foot on the top ladder rung and the other on the pool deck, she was exposed and easily accessible from behind. Heather held the top of the handrail with both hands. Her body was electrified. Lucas continued to massage her entire groin area, pausing occasionally to insert a finger deep into her silky smoothness. Heather arched her back toward

Lucas, and her entire body stiffened as she came once again. Her breathing was rapid, as if she'd never before experienced such a powerful orgasm. Heather remained in that position for a short while before she left the pool and retrieved her clothes.

"Lucas, I'm speechless. I had no idea sex could be so wonderful. You, my dear, have my number."

"We did just have a fantastic evening," Lucas said, "what with the dinner, the swimming, and the sex. When we look back on tonight, what do you think you will find most memorable?"

"Which time? The first time I came, the second, or the third? Just being silly, Lucas. Everything was fantastic: the sex was fantastic, you were fantastic, and the entire evening will be remembered forever."

"I tend to agree. Don't know about you, Heather, but I think I could fall asleep as soon as I hit the pillow. What do you say we make our way back to the apartment?"

"I'm with you. You wore me out tonight."

"I don't know, Heather, I think the wine may have had something to do with it."

"Nope, just you."

"When we get back to the apartment, want to try for four?"

"Lucas, you can't be serious. Are you trying to send me to an early grave?"

"No, just thought it may be a nice way to put a cap on the evening."

"Lucas, I've had a cap put on my evening, but thanks for offering."

Lucas and Heather retreated to the apartment, where they both settled in for a restful evening.

Lucas's plan began to unfold the following morning, when the two woke up and Lucas suggested they go out to breakfast.

"Good morning, big guy," said Heather as she rolled over to face Lucas. "What's on your mind? Gonna give me number four?"

"Can't. It has to be number one; too much time has passed for it to be number four. Besides, the little general feels a little under the weather this morning. What did you do to him last night?"

"Fucked him hard, that's what. It was a graduation fuck."

"No kidding. I thought we might go out for breakfast this morning. Where would you like to go? The choice is yours! You pick it."

"Let's go to Mama's. They always have good food and I like the warm atmosphere."

"Let's do it," responded Lucas. "Why don't you stay here and use the master bathroom, and I'll use the one in the hall? That way we should be finished at about the same time."

"I like the way you think, Lucas; finishing at the same time is a good thing."

About thirty minutes later, the two emerged from their respective bathrooms and headed for the door, Heather wearing the same clothes from their night out. She still looked elegant, although not as fresh, and was pleasantly flushed, feeling just a little naughty without panties. Lucas wore jeans, a blue polo shirt, and white running shoes.

Since Lucas's Corvette was still in the hotel parking lot, Lucas summoned a cab for the short trip to the restaurant.

Seeing the cab approaching the apartment, they both headed for the door. Lucas stepped out and turned to lock the patio door, while Heather held the sliding screen door, awaiting the opportunity to close it. Without delay, they headed straight to the awaiting cab. Being the gentleman he was, Lucas went straight to the rear door and opened it for Heather. As she scooted to the center seat, Lucas joined her. After buckling in, they were off to the restaurant.

Once seated, the only remaining duty was to decide on what to eat.

"What are you having today, Heather?" asked Lucas.

"Think I'll have my usual, the Southwest omelet," responded Heather.

"Sounds good; think I'll have the same. While we are waiting for our food, I have some things I want to share with you. First, you know I'll be going to Dallas in about four weeks and as I see it, things will be rather uncertain for me for the next six months to a year. I know this is going to come out of the clear blue, but I've given it lots of thought and I think you should see other people."

"What are you saying?"

"Heather, I don't know what kind of a future we are going to have together."

"Where is this coming from?" asked Heather as her eyes began to tear. "We get along wonderfully. I thought you liked me."

"I do like you, but there is a difference between liking someone and spending the rest of your life with that person."

"Lucas, I love you. What is causing this? Have you met someone?" she sobbed.

"No, I'm just not convinced that we are right for each other in the long run. If I am correct, why continue acting like we are?"

"I'm not acting. Are you?"

"I don't mean acting like that. I mean pretending to ourselves."

"I'm not pretending, Lucas. Have you been pretending?"

"OK. Let me start over. I don't know what my next six months to a year will look like. I will need to focus on my new job. I need to have one thing on my mind. Also, when I was thinking about us the other day, I realized that you wouldn't be happy with me—not in the long run. After realizing that, it made sense to cut our losses. If we're eventually going to go our separate ways, why not pull the plug now?"

"Cut our losses? Our losses, Lucas? Pull the plug?" Heather's voice changed from one full of hurt to one full of anger.

"It just seems like it would be best for both of us to go our separate ways."

"I don't think so, because I don't want to. How do you figure it's best for both of us? How do you know I won't be happy with you in five years? How do you know that? I thought our feelings for each other were mutual. I thought we were building on something."

"Heather, neither of us has made any commitments, and for whatever reason you don't seem content with who I am."

"Why would you say that? Do you think I go around fucking everybody?"

"Of course I don't think you sleep with everyone, but I say that because you always want to know more about me."

"Are you fucking crazy? This is because I want to know more about you? I don't see anything wrong with wanting to know more about the person I'm fucking every other night. I don't want to discuss this anymore. You made it clear that you're going to remain cloaked in secrecy."

"I'm not cloaked in secrecy. I don't want to argue with you. I don't want to hurt you, and I don't want us to part this way."

"Well we *are* arguing, this *is* hurting, and if you are telling me that we are going our separate ways, this is a shitty way to do it. What a fucking dramatic departure, saying good-bye over an omelet. Why did you allow me to think you actually cared for me? Is this what you were thinking last night when your dick was inside me? That wasn't a graduation fuck; that was a good-bye fuck."

"I do care about you. My feelings for you are the reason we're having this conversation."

"This isn't a conversation and I would hate to think of how this would go if you *didn't* have feelings for me." Heather's voice had grown loud enough that others began to notice.

"Heather, I guess I don't know how to tell you how I feel. You are a special person to me. I like you. Trust me, if I didn't care about you, I wouldn't be here this morning. I care about your feelings and I care about your future."

"Then you have a funny way of caring for people. I pity the people you don't care for."

"Just try to listen to what I'm saying. I will be living in my own little world for the next six months to a year, and won't be able to give you the attention I know you deserve. If I may be blunt, you would be ignored."

"Lucas, are you really that single-minded? I know other couples who've had significant events occur in their lives, and they didn't split up. I think there's more you're not telling me—or maybe you're not being honest with yourself."

"Heather, let's take a time-out and enjoy breakfast."

"So you think this is my destiny? Fuck breakfast. Fuck you. And by the way, I hope your dick falls off."

Heather got up and left Lucas still sitting at the restaurant.

The End